MYTHICAL MONSTERS

MYTHICAL MONSTERS

VAMPY VAMPIRES, ZANY ZOMBIES, & WACKY
WEREWOLVES +++

THE HORROR LITE SERIES
BOOK 3

ANGELIQUE FAWNS   MARK LESLIE

CATHERINE WEAVER   JENNY PERRY CARR

DELLA MARIE SULLIVAN

This book is dedicated to my mother, Della Marie Sullivan. She gives me the gifts of creativity, a never-ending supply of books, and free story editing.

CONTENTS

FOREWORD
MONSTERS ARE REAL AND THEY WALK AMONG US

BY MARK LESLIE

When Angelique Fawns offers you to take her literary hand and to walk with her down that dark moonlit path so she can share some tales with you, you immediately know you're in for much more than you bargained for.

For one, you'll begin to realize that monsters are not mythical. They're real.

Very real.

They live and breathe, they hunt and prey, they hide, they reach, they long, they lust.

They are as real as you and I, Dear Reader.

As real as the hopes, fears, and daily travails that we face every day.

But there is something uniquely compelling and satisfying as Angelique bends our ear and relays tale after tale to us. And we know that the stories she spins will live on long after the echoes of her voice on a cool night wind fade in the distance.

For the monsters, the creatures, the beasts she brought to life, will live on. We'll recall the nod to special "monstrous" days such as

Halloween and Friday the 13th. We'll appreciate both her take on werewolves and other classic allegedly mythical shapeshifting beasts along with creatures entirely of her own invention. We'll marvel at the twists on zombies and vampires, including one that sees them come together with romance, murder, and general mayhem in her hilariously entitled "What Slays in Vegas."

But more than anything, we'll be made to think deeply about just how universal and human most of those creatures are.

Because, like I said, they are us, after all.

Along her walk, she'll introduce you to a few friends.

Della Marie Sullivan will allow you to sink your teeth into a Romanian-style Halloween in her own atmospheric tale.

You might wonder if the beauty *is* the beast in the intriguing story from Jenny Perry Carr.

You'll be tempted by the tale of a siren collaborating with a water skeeter in a dark tale by Catherine Weaver.

And you may even spot me hiding in the woods along the path you walk, whispering a tale to beware of the shadowy creatures that lay waiting in the night.

Like I said, you're in for much more than you bargained for.

Now go ahead.

Angelique is patiently waiting.

Take her proffered hand.

And follow her into that dark and monstrous night.

Mark Leslie

October, 2023

1

———

ABOUT "A DEADFUL FRIDAY THE 13TH"

~

First broadcast: October 2021
Creepy Pod

THE ZOMBIE *in this medical thriller does NOT eat brains. What if there was a monster who made humanity better?*

2

———

A DEADFUL FRIDAY THE 13TH

BY ANGELIQUE FAWNS

I died on Friday the thirteenth. I wasn't superstitious before, but I sure am now. The omens were all there. A full harvest moon in October. Halloween Night. And it was Friday the thirteenth. Clearly not an auspicious time to be undergoing emergency gall bladder surgery.

I was helping my boys dress up as characters from the Walking Dead when the first pang hit me. A sharp piercing pain deep in my gut. I applied the last of their ghoulish makeup and asked my husband Louie to take them trick or treating in the closest subdivision. We lived on a country road about a half hour from town so I wouldn't have to worry about little visitors demanding candy. Too remote for the goblins and ghouls. Figuring a little lie-down would help my stomach, I grabbed a textbook to continue studying for my master's degree in psychology.

I was a stay-at-home mom with an honour's university degree, but had left my program ten years ago when I got pregnant with the twins. Now Liam and Levi were getting older and it was time to start a new chapter. Preferably one where I could help people.

I was making a few life changes. Going back to school and finally tackling the baby fat I'd put on and never managed to get rid of. The

3

high-fat low-carb diet was working wonders. Imagine losing 40 lbs by consuming fat, fat and more fat? Butter, bacon, cheese, and I was almost back in my high school jeans. Thirty was definitely the new twenty for me!

When Halloween falls on a school night it's always hectic trying to feed everyone before its time to hit the streets. Instead of cooking, we had a large pepperoni pizza delivered and we all pigged out. The oozy gooey mozzarella paired with spicy meat was hot and delicious, even if it did burn the roof of my mouth. My sons complained raucously because I ate just the toppings off, leaving the carby crust.

"Lena, that is so wasteful," Louie said.

Rushing to finish their pizza, the boys bundled up and zombie-walked their way to the car. Louie laughed at them.

"Good job dressing them in white, at least they are highly visible," Louie said following them them out.

That greasy pizza must have been the last straw for my overtaxed gall bladder. As soon as the guys left, I was over the toilet puking like a frat girl. The searing hot burning in my gut, torture.

After about an hour or so, my family returned. Laughing and arguing loudly over who had the biggest sugar haul. I felt too weak to even call out. The bathroom floor was cool on my fevered cheek and I figured someone would have to use the washroom shortly. Levi was the first one to finally walk in and see me on the floor.

"Liam! Dad! Mom's laying on the floor!"

Louie took one look at me and immediately called 911 on his cell phone. Liam, the more sensitive of my boys, grabbed a face cloth and soaked it in cold water. He laid in on the back of my neck.

"Mom are you okay Mom?" he asked.

"Oh my god Mom. What happened to you? The flu?" Levi also asked peeking from behind his brother.

I wanted to reassure them and tell them to go back to counting their candy, but I could hardly breathe with the pain. It was taking everything I had just to remain conscious.

"Forget the ambulance, I'm taking you myself," Louie scooped me up off the floor, and ran to his car, the twins trailing after us.

"Boys, stay here and mind the fort. I'll call you as soon as I know what's wrong with your..." Louie's voice faded as the intense agony of the jostling made me pass out.

When I came to consciousness, faces in masks were all I could see. I was being wheeled on a stretcher into surgery. The walls were blurry, and the acid burning in my stomach was overwhelming. I could smell that peculiar odour that is unique to hospitals; antiseptic mixed with the faint smell of urine.

"It's okay, we are going to take good care of you," a nurse with kind blue eyes said, "your gallbladder needs to be removed. It's full of stones and leaking bile."

As soon as they had me in surgery, the anesthesiologist knocked me out again. Then I was in the hands of the surgeon. Dr. Weinstein. And he wasn't having a good day. The man shouldn't have been making a sandwich, much less operating on someone. He had just been served with divorce papers an hour ago. His wife caught him cheating with their nanny. Instead of being focused on my laparoscopic cholecystectomy, he was completely distracted. Dr. Weinstein was furious he got caught.

Was he envisioning his wife with every slice in performed in my guts? Because he was a little too enthusiastic. He cut through my liver. He cut into my spleen. And he removed my gall bladder along with my cystic duct and my hepatic duct. Those he should have left alone.

Though I was supposed to be under anesthesia, I could hear the beep beep beep of medical monitors. Then the beeping stopped.

"We are losing her! Get the crash cart!"

Whomp.

"Again!"

Whomp.

Then peace and warmth. This dark place with light on the fringes. My life actually did flash before my eyes. The smile of my mother, my heart skipping a beat when I met Louie, the amazing smell of my twin boys the first time I held them.

Then a pain ripped through my chest and the warmth was gone. I heard the beeping again.

"She's back! We've got her back!"

"She's opening her eyes. Oh my god. What's wrong her eyes?"

I tried to make it back to that warm place but no luck. I hovered in and out of consciousness with a new feeling in my stomach. The burning had been replaced. I was hungry. Intensely... ravenously... hungry.

"Lena honey? It's Louie, please talk to me," my husband leant over, his sweaty hand gripping my cold one.

I slowly open my eyes and saw his blurry handsome face.

He gasped, "your eyes are white!"

I wanted to ask him to explain, but my vocal cords weren't working, I just sort of growled. Sort of like how my stomach was growling. This hunger was so intense.

A nurse walked in, "how are you feeling? The doctor successfully removed your gall bladder, but we had some complications during surgery."

"What kind of complications? Where is the doctor?" Louie asked.

I could see his face was pinched with worry, but he looked blurry. Hard to focus on. His hand was gripping mine tightly.

"She died on the table when her liver got punctured and she went into toxic shock. Officially she was gone for 15 minutes, but we brought her back. She's very lucky to be alive," the nurse said checking my IV bag.

"Dr. Weinstein should be in shortly."

I could hear rage in Louie's voice, "The doctor punctured her liver? Also, why are her eyes white?"

"She somehow grew ptergium, a mucous membrane that covers the cornea, during her time non-responsive on the table. It's not a.... common side effect," the nurse said.

She took a look at the heart monitor and tapped it in frustration. Rather than showing the steady peaks of a beating heart, it was flat, "this equipment is always malfunctioning, let me go get you another monitor," she left the room quickly.

I knew I should be in agony after having my insides stirred up like a chopped salad, but all I could feel was hunger. I had to eat something now. I opened my mouth to ask for a snack.

"Arggghhhhhhrrrrr," I said.

Sitting up, I ripped the IV out of my hand.

"Lena! What are you doing," Louie tried to gently push me back into the bed.

I grabbed his head with surprising strength and pulled him to me. I should have felt weak. With a deep intake of breath, I put my nose to ear and inhaled. I didn't want food, I wanted something else.

I sniffed his ear lobe again, one hand on his mouth to stop him from crying out. Nothing. Empty. I couldn't smell anything I wanted.

Shoving him aside, I stumbled out of the room, ignoring his gasp behind me. All my limbs felt stiff. I walked with a strange shambling gait. I had to eat.

I could vaguely tell that people in the hall were talking to me.

"Miss where are you going?"

"You shouldn't be out here!"

Ignoring them, I kept smelling the air, there was something tasty. Like a blood hound I was on a great scent. Getting to a door that said "staff only", I pushed it open. There he was. Dr. Weinstein. The surgeon that performed my surgery sitting in front of a computer typing furiously.

Bingo. My stomach growled and my salivary glands went into overdrive. He was so involved with typing up his report he didn't even turn to see who entered. Probably concocting some excuse for the botched surgery.

I shambled over and grabbed his head, one hand over his mouth. Pressing my nose to his ear, the most appealing smell leaked out. Like a damp chocolate cake. This is what I wanted, what I was hungry for.

Sucking as hard as I could, a black haze filtered out of his ear. I gulped it greedily. So tasty, this man's evil thoughts were decadent and filling. When there was nothing left, I let him fall back down into his chair. A dazed look on his face.

"I feel so good. Like someone took a huge weight off my shoulders. How could I have cheated on my beautiful wife? I am not going contest this divorce," he said.

"Ummmmm er," I said.

"In fact, I'll give her everything and volunteer for Doctors Without Borders. You have given me a gift. Thank you."

Louie was standing in the doorway watching with very wide eyes.

"Honey, did you just suck on that man's head?"

"Yumblooo," I answered.

Turning around, I stiff legged towards the door and Louie jumped out of my way. I was feeling a bit hungry again. Going down a flight of stairs and into the emergency waiting room, I could see a young man with a bullet wound being pushed in a wheelchair by an orderly. He was wearing gang colours, teardrop tattoos on his face, and red seeping through the bandage on his arm.

I stepped in front of them and stopped the wheelchair. Before the orderly could react, I grabbed the man's head and sucked out the black haze from his ear. They were scrumptious, these dark devious thoughts. Satisfying.

When I pulled back, he looked at me in wonder, "I think I am going to start a youth-at-risk program."

"Garrglegoo," I stumbled out the emergency room doors into the parking lot.

I was getting peckish again, and couldn't the world use fewer nasty people? This wasn't quite how I envisioned my role as a therapist, but sometimes your path chooses you. So many delicious nasty thoughts in the world. And I was so hungry.

3

———

ABOUT "THE SHADOW MEN"

First published: January 2009
Northern Haunts: *100 Terrifying New England Tales*

Mark Leslie is the reason I started this project in the first place. Settle in for his chilling tale of a camping trip gone wrong.

Mark Leslie is a writer, an editor, a professional speaker, and a book nerd with a passion for craft beer. He has published more than twenty-five books including thrillers and fiction (*Evasion, A Canadian Werewolf in New York, One Hand Screaming*), & paranormal non-fiction (*Haunted Hospitals, Spooky Sudbury, Tomes of Terror*).
https://markleslie.ca

4

THE SHADOW MEN

BY MARK LESLIE

I'll never forget the night that changed my life forever. It happened in the woods when I was ten years old.

It was dark; the air was crispy and chilly. Curious little sounds cut through the night—small animals rustling in the nearby bushes, the haunting call of a loon on the lake, leaves whispering in the breeze. And the air was charged with the smell of the still-burning embers of a recently doused campfire.

It was a night, in fact, not all that different than tonight.

I was sleeping in a four-man tent with my parents and younger brother and woke up with an overwhelming urge to pee. I crawled out of my sleeping bag, careful not to wake anyone else, slipped outside the tent and headed down the moonlit path to where I remembered the outhouse was.

Before I took more than a dozen steps I heard a noise behind me: the crack of a branch breaking underfoot.

With my hairs standing on edge, I managed not to let out a yelp as I turned.

There on the path not three steps behind me stood my little brother, a look on his cute button-nosed face like I'd just caught him sneaking a treat from the cookie jar.

"Jimmy," I whispered. "What are you doing?"

He stood with his right leg partially crossed over the left.

"Need to pee," he said, shifting his weight from foot to foot.

"Geez, Jimmy. If you had to go that bad, why'd you wait so long?"

"Because," he said, his six-year-old eyes wide and bright in the reflected moonlight, "the *Shadow Men* might get me."

I felt a shiver run down my spine despite the fact that I knew the *Shadow Men* were something my father had conjured up that evening around the campfire. They were the bogeyman of the New Hampshire wilderness that hid behind trees and lurked in the shadows. Their sole purpose was to trick little boys down the wrong path in the woods, deeper and deeper into the forest and far from the safety of their parents.

Even at ten, I knew my father told the story to use for fun and perhaps partially to keep us from wandering far away from them; but when Jimmy said that I still felt a chill.

"The *Shadow Men* aren't real, Jimmy."

"Are too! Listen!"

At just that moment the haunting call of a loon echoed through the forest, delivering a deep shiver up the base of my spine.

"That's just a loon," I said, but the chill wouldn't go away.

"No. Listen, Charlie. It's a little boy. One that the *Shadow Men* tricked. He's warning us."

Frustrated with my brother—and, okay, a little frightened—I just wanted it to end; I didn't want to hear any more. So I thought I'd throw a good scare into him.

I turned and ran down the path. "Jimmy!" I called out. "Behind you! The *Shadow Men* are behind you!"

He let out a cry. "Wait!"

Able to see the path clearly in the moonlight, I ran fast, took a sharp turn, and ducked down behind a low bush. Jimmy ran past me, still calling ahead on the trail for me to stop, panic rising in his voice as he seemed to think I'd gotten really far ahead of him. I had to put my hands on my mouth to suppress a laugh. But I stayed silent that way, listening to the padding of his footfalls on the packed dirt path and his calls for me to wait for him receding into the darkness.

His last cry was drowned out by the shrill call of a loon in the distance.

And I never saw him again.

But I hear him all the time.

Now, every time I'm out in the wilderness, out camping, I can hear my little brother's voice. Somewhere, masked within the sad, mournful, unearthly half-laughing, half-wailing cry of a loon, I can hear my little brother warning me that the *Shadow Men* are near.

Just listen for it and tell me what *you* hear...

5

ABOUT "WHAT SLAYS IN VEGAS"

~

First published: Sept 2023
Book Worms Issue 1

VAMPIRES MEET Zombies in a Vegas Casino. Put your money on an unlikely romance, murder, and general mayhem.

6

———

WHAT SLAYS IN VEGAS

BY ANGELIQUE FAWNS

Thana's stomach clenched in impatience as she watched her sister outline her lips in garish red lipstick. As usual, Drusilla was hoarding the bathroom mirror, her hips swinging to the jazz pouring out of the high-end hotel speakers. Only her 1940's ball-gown and beehive hairstyle hinted at Drusilla's true age. At 120-years-old, she was ravishing. No wrinkles. No blemishes. Not a hint of grey in the long black hair that hung to her waist.

"Why do you insist on using a mirror? It's not like you can see yourself." Thana tugged at her own spiky blonde hair.

Drusilla ignored her, also as usual.

"Let's club tonight." Thana tapped her foot to the music filtering up from the casino below. "I want to dance! Maybe nibble on some cute women for a change."

"Thana, do you ever give it up? What did our clergyman tell you? It's not natural to covet women." Drusilla swept into the sitting area.

Neon light flickered from the sliding glass balcony doors in the gaudy Vegas suite. Thana followed her, gnashing her teeth.

"You do know it's the twenty-first century? People can bite whomever they want."

"Maybe if you tried to look a little more feminine, you'd find it easier to glamour men." Drusilla wrinkled her nose at Thana's jeans and t-shirt.

Thana fingered the jade pills tucked in her jeans pocket. "I saw a great place to dance last night. The club has rainbow flags and a red wine drink special." She laced her fingers, pleading.

"I listened to you eighty years ago and look where it got me! If you hadn't dragged me out into the woods to meet that village girl..." Drusilla shook a fist. "Now I'm cursed."

Thana rolled her eyes. "Can you stop roasting that old chestnut? A girl makes one mistake and pays for it forever."

"My point, exactly." Drusilla walked to the bar to pour a glass of red wine.

"Seems to me you are living your best life. Being cursed suits you."

Drusilla flutters her long eyelashes. "Okay, so I don't mind eternal youth and perfect skin."

Thana sighs. "I bet you don't."

"Could you put something less butchy on? There's a lovely black dress in the closet. Show off those stocky gams of yours. I've ordered some room service."

A loud rap resonated on the hotel door and Thana opened it to a vision of beauty.

"Hi, I'm Jax, and I'm here with all sorts of tasty things!" The diamond in her nose twinkled.

Thana looked at the cart piled with oysters, strawberries and vodka bottles. Two men stood behind it, straight out of a stripping catalogue.

"You are the tastiest thing I see." Thana let her eyes take in Jax's tight uniform and curly red hair.

"I'm the bellhop. I just deliver the food and entertainment." Jax mock curtsied.

"Mantastic." Drusilla shoved Thana out of the way to pull in a dreadlocked man in leather pants.

Another swarthy fellow in a cropped tux took the cart from Jax and rolled in the booze and snacks.

Thana lingered at the door and smiled at the bellhop. "Can you join the party?"

"The casino might grind to a halt if I don't keep delivering sandwiches and shots. Anyway--" Jax nodded at the two stud muffins gyrating in the living room. "Not really my scene."

"She's not invited." Drusilla shoved a twenty-dollar bill into Jax's hand and slammed the door.

Thana clenched her teeth. "That was so rude--"

"Come meet Vinny and Jon, they can do the most delightful things with their pectorals." Drusilla cut her off.

Thana stalked to the couch. Vinny (he had his name tattooed on his neck) wiggled his crotch in her face. Thana gagged and pushed him away.

"Time for cocktails." She slunk around Vinny.

In the mini-kitchen she made four Cosmopolitans and slipped little jade pills into two of them. She saw Drusilla on the bed with Jon. She was removing his tuxedo and licking his neck.

"Let the guy have a drink first." Thana pushed her sister aside and put a Cosmo into Jon's hand.

"Cheers!" Jon took a sip as Drusilla pulled on his dreadlocks with her teeth.

Vinny was gyrating against Thana's bum. She shuddered and gave him his drink.

Vinny looked at her hopefully. "Got any coke?"

"Sorry, fresh out of blow."

Vinny winked and took a drink. "This will have to do."

He guzzled the entire cocktail. His eyes rolled up into his head and he collapsed on the couch.

"Thana, NO, not again." Drusilla threw Jon's empty cocktail glass at Thana.

Thana ducked and it narrowly missed her head, shattering against the wall.

Jon was slumped unconscious on the bed. Drool caught in his goatee.

Drusilla slapped Jon, trying to wake him up. "Why do you tranquilize them? It destroys the sport."

"Do we have to traumatize a generation of beefcakes?" Thana put a pillow under Vinny's head.

"I hate you more with every passing decade." Drusilla gnashed her fangs.

"Can we not evolve? We can eat and not leave a plasma footprint. Take the blood you need and I'll cover up the fang holes." Thana pointed to the makeup bag on the bedside table.

"We're hunters, not makeup artists." Drusilla glared at Thana. "I like the struggle. Fear makes the blood taste so much better."

Drusilla bit Jon's neck, kneading a pillow and moaning as she swallowed. Blood welled up around her mouth and dripped onto the white comforter.

Thana's stomach growled. She looked at Vinny. He was sleeping like a defenseless baby on the couch.

Drusilla's moaning reached a fever pitch. Thana was also hungry but she didn't want to feed on a testosterone hamburger when she wanted estrogen steak. Her stomach growled, so she sighed and approached Vinny.

She flipped him over, pulled off his pants, and located the artery at the back of his leg. Closing her eyes, she envisioned the bellhop.

Jax.

Her lovely smile, the red curly hair. The short skirt tickling firm quads.

Thana's canines extended.

She sunk her fangs into Vinny's popliteal artery, just behind his knee. Counting slowly, she took ten swallows. The half-naked man groaned and twitched his foot. With each salty swallow, she felt strength and a heavy sleepy feeling wash over her.

Nine... Ten.

She forced herself to stop feeding. She took some ice from the bar bucket and placed it over the small fang wounds. Gently, she covered the red holes with concealer from the makeup bag.

Drusilla was still lapping at Jon, slurping like she'd reached the bottom of a milkshake.

Thana pulled her sister off the dancer by her long hair. "Drusilla, don't kill him. We signed that contract before the Las Vegas nest allowed us to hunt here."

Drusilla's eyes were dilated. "I'm making myself a companion." Her chin was soaked in blood. She swiped at Thana with her nails.

"You've drained Jon dry. You can't turn someone if they're already dead." Thana danced out of the way of Drusilla's claws.

Jon wasn't moving. His skin was white. Dark circles under his eyes.

Drusilla tried to lift Jon into a sitting position, but he fell limply back onto the bed. She bit her wrist and held it over his lips. A few drops of blood dribbled onto Jon's teeth. It pooled.

Drusilla mashed her wrist against his mouth. "Drink, damn you, drink!"

Lumps were growing on his face. Pus-filled lumps.

"What's happening to Jon?" Thana raised her eyebrows. "I've never seen THAT happen before."

"What was in those pills?" Drusilla covered Jon with a blanket and gave her sister a suspicious look.

"I got them from a new guy." Thana wrinkled her nose. Jon smelt like old blue cheese.

"God, I need a drink." Drusilla rolled her eyes. "So much for creating a new guy for myself. I'm getting so tired of you. Good thing alcohol makes you less boring."

"You're not my idea of perfect company either. Straight and vicious. Nice combination."

Thana got the two Cosmos she'd made earlier. From another pocket of her jeans, she slipped an Anectine paralytic pill into her sister's drink. The jade pills were too dangerous.

Drusilla drained the drugged drink. "How will I make you pay for this transgression? If you weren't my sister, I'd have put a stake in your heart years ago."

Jon groaned and knocked his blanket to the floor.

"It worked! I may have a man to hunt with after all." Drusilla eyes lit up.

Jon staggered off the bed, his head at a strange angle. He lurched towards them like he was auditioning for a zombie movie.

"I don't think it worked." Thana flew to the back of the room.

Drusilla tried to follow, but stumbled, her coordination gone. Jon unhinged his jaw and bit her arm.

Drusilla screamed and collapsed on the rug. Her flawless face was wrinkled in rage.

"You drugged me!?" She slurred, crawling towards her sister.

Thana moved towards the balcony.

Jon grunted and let the hunk of Drusilla fall out of his mouth. He looked like a kid who'd just tried his first brussels sprout. Jon raised his nose and sniffed the air. He turned his head -sampling the room - until he found Vinny.

The neuromuscular agent was taking full effect and Drusilla was paralyzed on the carpet.

"I don't care who's older. You're not the boss of me anymore." Thana spat at her sister.

Jon was shuffling towards Vinny. Thana pushed the zombie man aside and slung Vinny across her shoulder. She ran to the balcony, dropped the unconscious dancer onto a deck chair and wrenched the sliding glass closed.

Jon tried to walk through the door. He scrabbled and drooled, his face smushed against the glass. He screamed unintelligibly.

"Not the brightest undead guy, are you?" Thana taunted. The cool night breeze felt good on her neck.

There was a knock on the hotel room door.

"Hello, are you alright in there? It's Jax."

Thana caught her breath.

Several more knocks. "I'm just going come in and get my room service cart."

Jon slowly turned his head and gibbered. Thana whacked on the glass door to get his attention. Jax walked into the suite and the door swung shut behind her.

Thana called from the balcony. "No, get out!" The thick glass door muted her.

Jax surveyed the chaos in the room. She didn't look towards the balcony. The bellhop's jaw dropped as she surveyed the blood soaking the bed. Drusilla moaned, twitching on the carpet.

Jon sniffed the air and shuffled towards Jax. Thana thumped again on the glass to get her attention, but the bellhop was focused on Drusilla.

"Ma'am, are you okay? I'll get help." Jax shook the paralyzed vampire's shoulder.

Jon shambled towards the bellhop and bit her shoulder. Jax flailed at the undead man and Jon grabbed her wrist and bit the artery. Blood spurted all over his bare chest.

Thana opened the balcony door and rushed over to Jax.

She shoved the zombie aside and sobbed. "Buzz off Chippendead."

Thana pulled the silk scarf out of her hair. She tied it around Jax's wrist, trying to quell the blood. The smell was coppery, enticing. Thana's fangs slid out but she fought the urge to lick Jax.

She gritted her teeth and pulled the bellhop onto the balcony. Jon had managed to grab a foot and was chewing on Jax's toes. Thana kicked him in the chest. Jon fell back into the hotel room as Thana yanked the balcony glass door shut.

She laid Jax down on the concrete. Even with the silk scarf, blood was gushing out of her eaten wrist.

"Vampires and zombies? Am I having a nightmare?" Jax blinked at Thana.

Thana's own eyes blurred with tears. She bit her wrist and put it over Jax's rosebud lips. The first few drops landed on her tongue and Jax swallowed feebly.

"That's it. Drink." Thana stroked her hair, shoving her wrist into the bellhop's mouth.

Jax stop sucking and closed her eyes.

"No." Thana gasped. "I am so sorry."

If she had a living heart it would be broken. Bile choked her throat and her shoulders shook from violent sobs. She looked around the balcony for a piece of wood to thrust into her own chest.

Nothing. Even the deck chairs were plastic.

She resolved to sit on this balcony until the morning sun fried her to a crisp. Stroking Jax's face, she cried more tears than she had in a century.

Thana kissed Jax's eyelids and they quivered. Then opened. Instead of brown they were a bright blue. Butterflies trembled in Thana's belly.

"Oh. That's a rush." Jax grabbed Thana's wrist and sucked with enthusiasm.

"Enough, I think that's enough." Thana pulled her arm away.

Where she was crying before, now she couldn't stop laughing. Her cheeks hurt with smiling. Color flushed into Jax's cheeks and her hair straightened and grew. Her zombie bite disappeared. Healed with fresh new skin.

"I'm feeling peculiar Thana. Why does – what's happening, oh, that hurts..." Jax's body jerked and quivered.

"It will be over soon, let it happen." Thana soothed.

She looked at the balcony doors. Jon was back, face pressed into the glass making fish faces. Drusilla was sleeping on the carpet.

Jax's features relaxed. The transformation was over. If she was beautiful before, now she was ethereal.

She sat up and kissed Thana. "I'm really hungry."

"Do you understand what just happened to you?" Thana kissed her back, stroking her thick hair.

"I'm dreaming?" Jax asked.

"You're not dreaming."

"I've seen a few vampire movies. Is Vinny a gift for me?" Jax nodded at the half-naked man sleeping in the deck chair.

Thana wrung her hands, indecisive.

"I'm soooo hungry." Jax put a hand on Thana's thigh and it tingled.

"We will have to teach you how to control your appetite. But this one time? Go for it Jax." Thana smiled.

Jax tried to bite Vinny, but only made little indents with her teeth. She looked at Thana, brows knit in confusion.

"Imagine he's your favorite Celesbian. Kristen Stewart, maybe?"

Jax raised one eyebrow and long glittering fangs slipped over her lips. She sunk her teeth into Vinny's neck.

Thana's own fangs ran out and pressed against her lips, but she couldn't join Jax in a snack. She had a bit of clean-up to do. Zombie Jon was still licking the glass, so she shoved him over.

"I'm sorry." Thana crushed his head between her hands and he collapsed on the floor. "We can't have zombies joining the vampires in Vegas."

She crouched next to Drusilla. "Sister, I love you, but you are on your own now. Go ahead and make yourself a vamp-man, I'm hanging with Jax now."

Drusilla blinked her lovely black eyes, still frozen and drugged on the carpet.

Jax joined her, wiping blood from her chin. "What now?"

"Our first date of course. I know of a great club. And it's lady's night."

The two vampires smiled at each other.

7

ABOUT "LYCAON'S LAST CONQUEST"

~

First published: December 2022
The Fifth Di...

ONE OF THE *most common shapeshifters in speculative literature is the Lycanthrope — or werewolf. This story reinvents the Greek mythological character Lycaon, throws in some parental alienation syndrome, and imagines him in the midst of a modern-day love story.*

8

LYCAON'S LAST CONQUEST

BY ANGELIQUE FAWNS

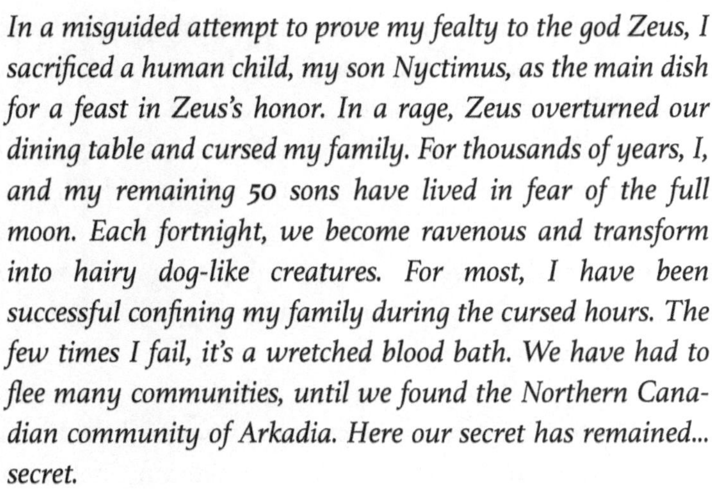

In a misguided attempt to prove my fealty to the god Zeus, I sacrificed a human child, my son Nyctimus, as the main dish for a feast in Zeus's honor. In a rage, Zeus overturned our dining table and cursed my family. For thousands of years, I, and my remaining 50 sons have lived in fear of the full moon. Each fortnight, we become ravenous and transform into hairy dog-like creatures. For most, I have been successful confining my family during the cursed hours. The few times I fail, it's a wretched blood bath. We have had to flee many communities, until we found the Northern Canadian community of Arkadia. Here our secret has remained... secret.

From the Diary of Lycaon

*L*ycaon crouched in the mud behind the large oak tree, his knees aching, as the full moon illuminated the forest trail. His silver coat kept him warm even though he could see his breath hanging in the cool spring air. Arkadia was an Acadian settlement in the far north of Ontario and summer came slowly. He should have been locked up tight in the barn with his furry, frolicking pack of kids, but Helix had snuck out. Always getting into trouble that one. Being an old werewolf was over-rated and nothing like the books or movies. Being thousands of years old wreaked havoc on the joints.

He could still appreciate beauty though, and the lady walking down the forest path was worth a wolf-call. Partha lived in town, sang at the local pub, and worked as a dog walker. Lycaon loved how her dark ponytail bobbed. She had the dark skin and dramatic cheekbones common in this culturally-mixed settlement. He wagged his tail in time with her hips as she gyrated them to whatever tune was playing in her headphones.

Lycaon was too shy to introduce himself. Why would a youthful blossom be interested in an old dog? His days of romancing woman were over. When they first settled in Arkadia, he'd gone a few dates with the owner of the local spa, Athena. It was hard to guess her age, she spent so many hours in her tanning bed, but if he had to guess he'd say pushing 70. She crackled with energy and sexuality, but when Lycaon tried to take their relationship to the next step, Athena had shut him down, "I've kept my virginity up to this point, so I'm not going start spreading'em now."

Lycaon still liked to get a leg over, but that wasn't the reason he left her. They had a fight over the colloidal silver baths at her spa.

"Look Lycaon, it's a cure-all, good for skin and helps arthritis," Athena had insisted. "My clients love it. I'm not draining my pools for you."

A bath in silver. Not the best idea for a werewolf. Even if that water splashed up on him, it could be fatal. He broke up with Athena. His hands were getting tired anyways from all the massages she demanded. Plus, it felt deceitful dating her when he was really enamored with the alluring dog-walker. He never missed any of Partha's performances at the pub, that girl could sing. He'd even contemplated buying a dog, just so he could pay her to walk it.

Helix had also been sniffing around Partha, but she'd turned down his advances. His son was good-looking in a bearded, man-of-the-woods kind of way, and had a reputation as a ladies' man. This was the first time Helix, or any of his sons, had escaped the barn on the night of the full moon. He would be a true "lady killer" if Lycaon didn't stop him.

Lycaon was careful not to shift position in case an errant twig crunched under his paws. He didn't want to alert the Partha's dog. A white snack of a terrier, complete with studded pink collar.

Even with the insulation of his fur, a shiver ran through him. As the temperature dropped with the sun, he could smell the cold. At least Partha was dressed for the weather. Tight acid wash jeans, and a red flannel shirt. Plaid of course, jokingly called the "Arkadia Dinner Jacket" by locals. Lycaon licked his jowls as she danced to her silent music. It took him many decades of mediation, but he could control his moon-fueled blood lust. She was almost directly in front of him when his cruciate ligaments quit. He fell onto his face, managing to suppress a quick yip of pain.

More than a few twigs crunched.

The terrier erupted into high-pitched yapping while yanking Partha to the side of the path. Lycaon held his breath, his chin an inch into the dirt, and tried not to move a muscle. Good thing he had a thick silver muzzle, or he'd have some serious road rash on his face. The sinking sun was on his side and kept him hidden in shadow.

"Hey Tootie, keep my arm in its pit, please!" Partha regained her balance, making the terrier sit.

The dog sniffed at a fanny pack looped around her waist.

"Okay, nummies for a numbskull," she pulled a milk bone out of the neon green bag.

With the dog distracted, Lycaon let out the breath he was holding. A mushroom was stuck to his whiskers. He inhaled the nutty, toasty aroma. Morels! Spring was the best time to harvest them. He loved making mushroom soup. He nibbled on a few, even keeping a few tucked in his cheek for the flavor. Lycaon slumped his nose deeper into the soil. Farming was something he could at least understand in this day and age. All that tech stuff confounded him, so he fed his pack of ravenous sons with home grown produce.

He liked it here in Arkadia. The predominately Acadian, Metis, and Indigenous population were welcoming, but very private. Distrustful of government authority, this community self-regulated, which was perfect for his unconventional family. Moving would be so disruptive if they were run out of town.

Thankfully, Partha was on the move again, and he focused on her instead of contemplating depressing "what ifs". Twerking and dancing, she continued down the path, fanny pack slapping her rump. He could see her little red Jeep parked 400 feet away on the road bordering the woods. Lycaon got his haunches under him and took a few cautious steps through the underbrush, reluctant to let her out of sight.

He smelt his son's overactive pheromones seconds before he slithered out from the other side of the trees. Helix's black coat was coarse and stuck up like porcupine quills along his spine. His fangs were dripping saliva.

"Well, hello delicious," Helix reared up on his hind legs and blocked Partha's path.

She screamed but quickly recovered, fumbling with her fanny pack. The zipper refused to open, "Damn it, I knew I shouldn't have bought this from the Dollarz store."

The chuckle rumbling from Helix turned to a growl when Tootie launched herself at him. He swatted her aside like a pesky mosquito and the little white mop flew through the air.

"Pick on a puppy your own size," Partha assumed an odd karate stance, "you picked the wrong lady, dog breath," She kicked at Helix's ribs.

Helix caught her foot with one huge paw and threw her to the ground. Her head hit the ground with a sick thud. Lycaon's teeth chattered in panic. Could he beat the younger werewolf in a fair fight? Helix was a rebellious lad and he might slay his father without a second thought. He wanted to be Alpha. Bile rose to Lycaon's throat watching him lick Partha's bloody forehead.

"I told you, you picked the wrong lady, flea bag" Partha lurched to a sitting position, slapping and kicking.

"You should have said yes when I asked you to dinner last week. This date will be shorter, but far tastier," Helix stood over her.

She grabbed his ears and smashed her forehead into his snout.

"You bitch," blood spurted from Helix's nose, and he raised a paw, ready to swipe her head off.

Lycaon couldn't procrastinate any longer. He launched, his joints cracking in protest. With hackles high, his claws extended, he landed on his son's back.

"Bad dog," he growled as the both of them rolled off Partha.

Lycaon was a bigger wolf than his son, and his jaw hit the center of the black werewolf's skull. Helix's eyes rolled back into his head and he slid to the ground, unconscious. As with all werewolves; when they approach the brink of death, he transformed back into a young man. He laid on the side of the path, naked and still.

Partha was breathing hard. She looked up at Lycaon and then at Helix, "That guy! I knew he was a dog. I just didn't mean it literally."

Lycaon looked at Helix's chest, he could see it rising and falling. His wild child would survive.

"Am I having a nightmare?" Partha asked.

"I can explain if you can keep a secret-" There was a wild rustling in a fern patch. The little terrier rushed out and bit Lycaon's hock.

"Hey!" Lycaon shook his leg, trying to dislodge the growling ball of fur.

Tootie hung on, snarling and drooling. Her mouth was too little to grab more than just his thick muddy fur.

Partha groaned, "Tootie, you won't win this fight, let go."

She reached one trembling hand to her forehead and wiped away a bit of blood. Tootie renewed her attack on Lycaon's ankle.

"Hell, when I wake up for real, I'm putting some Baileys in my coffee," Partha staggered to her feet, put her fanny pack back on, and removed the little dog from the old werewolf's ankle.

Lycaon laid down on the path and rolled over onto his belly in a non-threatening posture, showing his old spotted skin. Partha looked down at him with wide, confused eyes.

"I can keep a secret. But hey, you know what I'm worried about right now? What the hell were you doing in the bushes?" Partha finally got the zipper to open on her fanny pack, and took an evil looking taser out and pointed it at Lycaon. He rolled back over, eyeing the weapon cautiously.

"Mushrooms," Lycaon said, his ears drooping.

"What?"

"Eating mushrooms," he said again, dropping the half-chewed fungus he'd kept in his cheek on the ground.

A bit of blood trickled into Partha's eyebrow and her nose crinkled. She jabbed the weapon at him. A zap and spark of electricity. She was inches from touching him.

"Okay, the mushrooms might not be the whole truth. I was trying to keep Helix, my son, out of trouble," Lycaon nodded to the passed-out man on the trail.

"Your son who was a wolf, but is now naked and passed out over there," Partha pointed at Helix.

"I'm sorry about the little scallywag, we might be having a few Alpha issues. He needs to learn how to court by taking a lady out for dinner, not eating them for dinner." Lycaon, tried to grin, showing a full mouth of sharp teeth.

"What are you? Werewolf? Demon?" Partha waved her taser.

"I'm Lycaon. A werewolf one night a month, but most of the time a man of the land. From the farm over there," he flicked one ear towards the direction he came.

"You're the father of all those boys? They cause havoc in the bars. Good looking trouble-makers." Partha put the taser back in her fanny pack.

The butterflies in Lycaon's stomach swirled. She was so beautiful. Even now, bedraggled, shocked, and that delicious blood on her forehead. *"Don't think about the blood,"* Lycaon admonished himself.

His loins grew warm, he could have more sons with this lovely lady.

"Perhaps I could take you out for a coffee tomorrow? You'll find me a very civilized companion in my normal form," he asked, the old mojo flowing for the first time in centuries.

Partha's cheeks flushed, but she was saved from answering when Helix scuttled to his feet and took off into the trees.

"Hey, get back here you mongrel," Partha pivoted to go after him, but Lycaon blocked her way. Partha wasn't just beautiful. She was brave. Or really crazy. Probably both.

"Let my son go, even in human form he can be dangerous, and you are off the menu," he placed a paw gently on her chest.

"Why am I even thinking of going for coffee with you? God, I wish I was a cat lady," Partha shrugged him off, picked up Tootie, and stalked towards her car.

Lycaon stood there, panting and exhausted. He let her go, an old fart like him had no chance with a woman like that. Metis women were fierce. The last bit of sun dropped behind the horizon. He'd better get back to the farm before his other sons got themselves into trouble.

Lycaon stalked through the underbrush. He hated being a werewolf, but he did enjoy the night vision and heightened sense of smell. Fermented leaves, old bones, long dead carcasses, better than any perfume. The sky was hosting a real show tonight with a red orange glow in the northern sky. Lycaon paused... in the northern sky? The sun set in the west. For an ancient hound, this was the second time he found himself running full-tilt.

He could smell it before he saw it. The acrid smoke. He vaulted over his barn gate. The barn was on fire. Hungry flames reached towards the sky. Rays of moonlight darkened with waves of black smoke. The barn that housed all his sons.

The heat reddened his cheeks and the air burned his nostrils as he ran through his back field. The entire building wasn't involved yet.

Maybe he could save them. Frightened howls combined with the roar of the flame.

"Lycaon! Help me!" A panicked female voice.

Lycaon came to abrupt, panting stop. The barn and his family in one direction. The beguiling Partha in another. Someone had dumped a bushel of his firewood around his tall, ornate birdhouse and ignited it. Partha was struggling on the wood pole. The bonfire slowly eating its way up the pile of wood.

Why didn't he make sure she got safely to her car?

The flames were growing faster by the second. She had minutes before the fire reached her running shoes. Her legs were tied to the birdhouse.

Lycaon changed course and charged towards Partha. He catapulted straight up the woodpile into the fire. His thick fur prevented him burning right away. Partha's red-rimmed eyes met his and he gave her cheek a quick lick.

"I've got you; you're going to be okay," Lycaon gnawed through the bailer twine holding her to the birdhouse pole.

Partha tumbled forward, grabbing the scruff of his neck, and Lycaon carried her out of the bonfire. Coughing and choking, Partha got up and ran towards the barn, now really roaring with flame. Lycaon followed, galloping behind her. He looked in distress at the lock on the door, he couldn't open it with his paws. Partha took off her jacket, wrapped it around one hand, and turned the lock. Then she yanked open the door, falling back from the licking flame. They both had to step back from the searing heat while peering into the smoke. Nothing.

"I'm so sorry Lycaon," Partha said over the roar of the flames. She shook her head.

Loud screaming pierced the air and a melee of naked boys ran out the door. A few red embers were caught on the thick, wiry hair of their transforming skin, but miraculously they seemed relatively unharmed.

"Dad! Thank god," one tow-headed boy hugged his neck.

"We were going to be barbecued," a dark-haired wiry boy leapt on his back.

More kids piled on, but Lycaon growled and shook them off ferociously.

"There is a lady here! To the house and get some clothes on!"

The boys ran while chattering excitedly towards the enormous old house. Lycaon and Partha watched as the barn folded in on itself with a loud crack and the flames reached for the sky.

"I'm sorry. If you didn't have to save me, maybe you could have saved the barn," she squeezed a handful of fur on his neck.

"I would rather lose every building on this farm then see one hair on your head harmed," Lycaon rubbed his head against her stomach. "I should have made sure you were safe in your car. I'm the one who's sorry. How did you end up here?"

"Helix surprised me when I was putting Tootie into her crate in the back of my Jeep. He had me trussed and tied before I could get my zapper out."

"Did he bite you?" He asked gritting his own teeth.

"No. If he bites me when he's human, can he still give me lycanthropy?"

Lycaon just nodded.

"Let's get Tootie out of the car," Partha grabbed the little dog then asked, "Why would your son set fire to a barn full of his brothers?"

"He's always been a very jealous boy," Lycaon looked at the smoldering embers of his barn. "I guess he was eliminating his competition. There's always one who wants to challenge the Alpha.

Partha brushed some soot off her lips and winked, "I'm so tired, I'm not sure I can drive anywhere tonight."

"We have an apartment in the carriage house," Lycaon nodded towards a quaint building across the driveway from the main house. Was she just getting dirt out of her eye? Did she really wink at him? "You should have a shower and spend the night."

She followed him to the old wood stable and opened a side door. The inside, originally two horse stalls and a large central area to store a wagon, had been renovated into a cute studio apartment with a double bed and mini kitchenette.

"Forget the shower" Partha collapsed fully clothed onto the bed.

She was snoring in minutes and Lycaon thought about going back to the main house, but knew his sons would be noisy and unable to sleep after the excitement of tonight. Instead, he gingerly laid down beside Partha as Tootie curled up at the foot of the bed.

In the morning, Lycaon opened his eyes, naked, and fully human. He was glad he woke up before Partha. He didn't want her to think he'd been inappropriate. Wrapping a quilt around his waist, he ran his fingers over her dark hair resting on the pillow. The first rays of sun were catching dust motes around her face. It had been far too long since he had a beautiful woman in his bed. What a woman. She'd been attacked in the forest, abducted, and then nearly burned to death. All the while never shedding a tear. She'd even saved his boys by opening the barn door when he couldn't.

He could spend all morning gazing at her, but Helix was still out there. Werewolves behaved badly. It was their nature. But his sons had been raised to be behave when human. Helix had tried to kill his brothers and Partha after he transformed back. This was definitely not good. He really didn't want to have to find a new town, Arkadia had been perfect for them. Getting dressed quietly, he put a little note beside her pillow.

Had to go somewhere. Sorry. Talk later. Lycaon.

He set the coffee maker to brew some fresh java for her, found some coveralls and a sweater in the closet, then made his way to the archery range at the back of his property. Grabbing a quiver with small wood arrows from the shed, he assumed a shooting stance and nocked an arrow on his bow, slowly drawing it back. He focused on his target; a large cardboard bullseye propped up on a hay bale. Taking a deep breath, he released the bow. The whistle of the arrow sang in his ears as it flew away from him....

It missed the not only the bullseye, but the entire piece of wood, disappearing into the woods behind it.

"Watch out!"

Lycaon whirled around, knocking himself in the head with his bow. Partha was there, pointing at a dark creature beyond the bullseyes by the tree line.

Dark and ominous, it looked like a black bear was staring at them.

"That's a 3D archery target. There are a bunch of them," Lycaon pointed to the deer, coyote, and turkey sitting in the woods. "How did you find me?"

Partha grinned and pointed at his footprints in the melting snow, "Got to get up early to fool me."

She was dressed in the same plaid shirt as yesterday, but had pulled on a puffy vest and red toque from the carriage house closet. The vest hung to her knees, and her fluffy dark hair stuck out enthusiastically from under the hat. His heart raced, she looked adorable.

She looked him up and down, "Aren't you the silver fox? Or should I say silver wolf?" Lycaon couldn't think of a good comeback. She was flirting with him! Was he ever rusty. How did he manage to father 50 sons again?

What are you doing?" she asked.

"Helix has gone bad," he said, all business. "We can't let him live until the next full moon. A fully grown werewolf like him could take out this entire town in a night."

"You're going to shoot him with an arrow?"

Lycaon nodded, walked to his shed, and pulled out another quiver full of arrows, but these had oversized metal heads. He handed them to Partha.

"Now I get it. These arrows have silver tips," she expertly nocked an arrow into the bow and then let fly. She smiled when it hit the bear target dead center in the forehead.

"You're full of surprises." Lycaon said.

"Arkadia archery champ in high school. Five years running. My father was a pretty good shot. He taught me."

"Do I know your dad?"

"His friends call him 'Paulo', he travels a lot with his band," Partha let another arrow fly and decapitated the foam turkey.

"Paulo? As in Apollo? I guess music and archery run in the family," Lycaon shook his head. Who else from his past was hiding in plain sight in Arkadia?

"Why not a gun with silver bullets?" Partha demolished his fake raccoon high up in a birch tree.

"That's a false bit of lore. Bullets don't work. Not a big enough piece of silver." Lycaon strode out of the archery range.

Partha hurried after him, slipping her crossbow and quiver over her shoulder. "So, what's the plan?"

"Arkadia archery champ, eh? Could you get Helix in the chest with a silver arrow? He's probably going to come after you again, even before he turns. That boy doesn't take no for an answer." Lycaon helped Partha back into her jeep. Tootie already in her crate.

"Alright, I'll meet you at the forest parking lot at dusk," Partha said. "If Helix knows my routine, I dog walk there every night."

She slid into the driver's seat as Lycaon loaded the silver-tipped arrows and extra bow into the back of her Jeep. He was careful not to touch the tips. "I won't drive. That might alert Helix if he sees my farm truck parked by yours. I'll be hiding in the exact same spot as last night?"

"Hiding, Lycaon? I knew you weren't just picking mushrooms. It might have been easier to ask me out for coffee," she laughed and drove away.

Lycaon could feel his ears turn red.

That evening, dressed all in black, Lycaon made his way to the oak tree. He could see Partha across the path, up another oak on one of the old hunting stands. She was lying on her belly with the bow positioned so she could keep an eye on the trail. Her dark hair under a black ball cap, and the rest of her covered in green and brown camo spandex. The wood planks supporting her weight looked rotten, rain-soaked countless times.

Lycaon caught the edge of his cheek with his teeth, looking at her tense muscles ready to strike. She gave him a slight nod. Embarrassed, he concentrated on the surrounding woods. They both remained motionless as the sky darkened, the wind rustling the leaves, and a crow scolding in the higher branches. A coyote stopped a few feet away from Lycaon to mark his territory before slinking off in search of dinner. If he'd been in werewolf form, he would have snapped the coyote's neck for such rudeness.

A brown mule came around the bend carrying a slender man dressed in an Australian outback slicker and cowboy hat. It took Lycaon a few minutes, but then he recognized Helix. He must have borrowed the mule from a friend to help him hunt Partha.

Partha recognized the mule rider at the same time as Lycaon and let her arrow fly. It pierced Helix in the arm. He screamed and fell off the mule, frantically trying to pull the silver tip out of his arm. The mule reared up with a bray and bolted down the trail.

How could Partha miss his heart? Lycaon was able to defeat his son as a werewolf. But what about as a man?

Partha dropped from the stand and strode over to Helix. She was nocking another arrow into her bow when Lycaon saw someone else slink out from the trees. She had fly-away pink hair, an unbelievably dark tan, and a million facial wrinkles. Athena. What was she doing out here?

Lycaon froze. This was going all wrong. Partha looked at the older lady, scrunched her face in confusion, and pointed her bow at the ground. Athena grabbed her arm and dragged her away into the bushes.

Helix massaged his injured arm and slapped Partha's bum, "you crazy bitch, you ruined my arm."

Athena snarled at Helix, "Don't behave like a mutt."

The old lady was dressed in a faux fur jacket striped like a zebra and whirled on Partha, "Now Parthenos, you know better than wandering around the woods at night!"

"But-"

"Not a word! You are coming back with me."

Lycaon pulled on his beard, still hidden on the other side of the path.

What just happened? Partha knew Athena?

The wiry old lady pulled branches off an ATV hidden in a patch of greenery. Helix was kicking stones like a frustrated toddler, and Partha's head hung as she waited to straddle the ATV.

Lycaon could feel his breath coming in quick gasps, and his fists clenched. He didn't know what to do. So, he did nothing. Athena drove off with Partha sandwiched between her and Helix. When they were out of sight, Lycaon ran back to his farm. Athena's business, the Sun & Silver Spa, was on the other side of town. He prayed to Zeus that they were taking Partha there. It featured tanning beds and those horrid colloidal silver baths.

Home in minutes, he fought the urge to leap immediately into his pickup and roar to the spa. A smart man goes into the den of his enemy (or ex-girlfriend) with some back-up.

Opening the front door of the old farm house he could hear music, the twangy sound of a video game, and an enthusiastic belching contest. He shook his head. Boys will be boys, especially when you have so many of them. The closest kid to him, a teenager wearing an argyle sweater, and thick glasses was reading a book, 'Practical Pole Building Construction' on a couch in the front sitting room.

"Linus, get your brothers and head over to the Sun & Silver Spa as fast as our Harvester International Tractor can go. Hook up and load everyone up in the biggest hay wagon."

Linus pinched his glasses and scowled, "I'm almost done this chapter, do I have to?"

"Yes! Now," Lycaon was glad he had one cerebral kid. Linus wanted to be an engineer.

Arkadia was a small town and it didn't take Lycaon more than 20 minutes to get to the Sun & Silver Spa. Sitting just up a hill with extensive landscaping, the log building managed to look rustic and expensive at the same time. Athena's ATV was parked outside the glassed-in gazebo for the indoor pool.

Lycaon clenched his fists, took a deep breath, and pushed open the glass door onto the pool deck. A bare-chested Helix was lounging in a chair by the side of the pool icing the arrow wound on his shriveled arm. Athena was standing beside the pool, dressed in a lacey blue pool coverup, watching someone swim.

Partha was doing laps in the viscous water and her skin glowed with tiny bits of silver. She was swimming in a pool of colloidal silver.

"What's going on here?" he asked, scratching his head.

Partha pulled herself halfway out of the pool like a seal and grinned at him, "Hey Lycaon."

Helix got up and put his uninjured arm around Athena, "I'm dating this fine old piece of ass. She doesn't want me sniffing after her niece."

Athena spun from under Helix's arm and pushed him into the pool.

His scream hit a register a second soprano would be proud off. The bits of silver in the water made his flesh bubble like a bath balm.

Partha launched herself out of the pool before blobs of Helix could reach her, "Aunt Athena that's gross, you could have warned me!"

She grabbed a towel off of one of the lounge chairs and slipped her hand into Lycaon's. Trembling, he watched his son sink beneath the pool surface, his body dissipating like an Alka Seltzer.

"Lycaon, you got to control these boys of yours," Athena nodded at the red puddle in the pool.

Conflicting emotions warred on his face. Relief, shock, betrayal, confusion.

"That particular puppy of yours went feral," Athena continued. "He had to be put down for the good of the pack. Too bad, he was good at massaging my-"

A loud commotion outside. A big red tractor was chugging up the hill pulling a wagon with young men hanging off the sides, hooting and thrusting axes, chainsaws, and shovels in the air. Linus hopped from behind the wheel and walked towards the pool. Lycaon was relieved for the interruption. He didn't want to hear about Helix and what he was rubbing with his ex-lady friend. He supposed he should thank Athena for taking care of Helix. At least he didn't have to make a murderer out of the lovely Partha or kill the boy himself.

"I got 'em Dad. What's this about?" Linus's cheeks were flushed and his glasses tilted.

Lycaon went out to calm down the feisty pack. His sons were always up for a rumble.

"First off, stay out of the pool. Wait one second, I got a bit of business to take care of," Lycaon cupped his hands and drew from his diaphragm to be heard.

Athena and Partha joined him on the grass. The spa owner shaking her pink head in amusement and Partha snacking her arms around Lycaon's waist.

"I forgive you for killing Helix, Athena," he said leaning into her ear. He didn't want his remaining sons to know about Helix yet, he'd break the news to them another day. "I was trying to put him down myself. But we got ourselves a situation here. My barn was burned to the ground and in 28 days this whole town's going to have a problem."

Lycaon looked at his boys. Pallas was chasing Eumon around with a chainsaw. Leon, Phineus, and Ancyor were having an axe throwing competition. The Sun & Silver Spa was surrounded by an immense grove of hardwood trees. Maple, birch, aspen, cedar. All could work for building a new barn.

"Athena, can we do some logging in your wood stand?"

"I see where you are going with this, you old dog. Great idea. Yup, them woods could use some thinning out. I'm not going mind supervising all those young strong bodies," Athena did a little dance, "I'm going to get my lumberjack outfit on."

Lycaon shuddered. He wanted to get out of her before he found out what Athena thought a predatory lumberjack should wear.

"Linus! You ready to be a foreman? Get your brothers together and log some wood out of this forest. We're going to have ourselves an old-fashioned barn raising."

"Yes sir!" His son scampered off to organize his brothers.

Lycaon dropped to one knee in front of Partha who popped her eyes open in alarm when he took her hand.

"Partha, I know I might be an old wolf, but I'm in love with you. You are fierce and talented. I just lost myself a son and wouldn't mind having a few more. Will you marry me?"

She dropped to her knees so she was eye-to-eye with him.

"Lycaon, we haven't even gone on a real date yet. I like you, but I'm not going to marry you and I'm definitely not going to pop out more sons for you," she stroked his cheek. "I'm on the birth control pill, I've got a job, and my own apartment. I am willing to hang out. Maybe Netflix and chill."

Lycaon got to his feet and pulled her up with him. Looking furtively around, he was glad to see his sons were too busy attacking Athena's wood stand to have noticed his failed proposal.

"What is Netflix?"

Partha laughed, leaning forward to give him a long slow kiss. "You'll find out. Now I've got dogs that need walking."

Lycaon brushed his lips with one hand. They were stretched in a huge grin. He watched her straddle the ATV and roar down the road.

I had to sacrifice another child, and my heart does hang heavy. But the new love of my life is a wonderful salve to my soul. She is the human daughter of Apollo, and niece of that strange spinster Athena. Partha and I have grown close over the past few months. I have noticed her belly is growing. Perhaps I will once again have 50 sons? Thanks be to Zeus, the newly constructed barn has held strong, and the citizens of Arkadia remain safe. And our secret? Remains a secret.

From the Diary of Lycaon

9

ABOUT "HIGH ADVENTURE"

~

First published: April 2021
Econoclash Review #7

FAIRY, *Faery, Fairie, Faerie, Fayrie, Fhairy, Phhaerryyee, Fae, Fay, Faye, Faeye, Phae, are all acceptable ways to spell Fairy. There are also many different subgenres of fae. This story introduces us to an entirely new species. "The Rasta Fairy."*

Note that this version is dramatically different from the one that went to print.

10

HIGH ADVENTURE

BY ANGELIQUE FAWNS

Jolene struggled along the forest path on her crutches and almost tripped over the turtle shell.

"Wouldn't that be great, break my other ankle," she cursed to the sky.

She picked up the ridged orange and brown shell and flipped it over.

Jolene gasped.

There was a tiny lady flapping inside the smooth walls. Smoke oozed out of her nostrils, the smell of skunk heavy in the air.

She poked her stubby cigarette at Jolene. "Jeezum Pees, you're bothering me." Her shiny black, yellow and green dress bounced off tiny knees as she flapped her iridescent wings.

Jolene instinctively cupped her palms as the lady tried to fly by her.

"Whaddya think you're doing?" The musical voice was muffled by Jolene's hands.

She felt a sting as the wee cigarette was ground into one of her fingers.

"Ow! Stop that! Are you some kind of fairy?"

The little woman grinned; her teeth white against her dark skin. "I'm not just any fairy, I'm a Rasta Fairy."

Jolene opened her fingers a smidge. "A Rasta Fairy? I'm Jolene. Do you have a name?"

"I'm Kaleisha." The fairy coughed. "Kill me dead, I'm hotboxing myself in here. Let me go."

"Do you promise not to fly away?"

"Do I have a choice, giant girl?"

Jolene cracked her fingers a tiny bit more. "I might clap my hands together and mush you by mistake if you startle me. Neither of us wants that."

The fairy coughed again. "Alright give me some air."

Jolene opened her palms, and Kaleisha, true to her word, didn't fly away. But her pretty face was screwed up and her long braids swung as she hovered.

She gnashed her teeth. "Do you have snacks? I have a hankering for Mexican."

Jolene's face lit up. "I have Taco Bell in the fridge back home from last night!"

Kaleisha kicked at the air. "How that be helping me here?"

Jolene giggled at the little tantrum. "Do you grant wishes? I'd love this damn ankle fixed." She gestured to her cast.

"Look sister, I'm no Genie. Anyways, it's stupid to ask for yuh leg fixed. It's gonna heal. Ask for something worthwhile."

"I want to be a YouTube star," Jolene said.

"That's dumb. My big wish? A condo in the city and a burrito. I'm sick of flower nectar." Kaleisha pointed to a tree behind Jolene. "Hey look, Bigfoot!"

When Jolene looked over her shoulder, Kaleisha gave her forearm a good solid bite and flew into the trees.

"Ow!" She swiped at the fairy, but missed her by a mile. "Dang it. No one is going to believe this without proof." Kaliesha was nowhere to be seen.

She tucked the turtle shell into her pocket and limped down the trail. River water gurgled below her. Jolene should have been watching where she put her crutches instead of the sky. She lost her balance and rolled down the embankment. Flexing her fingers and toes, she sighed in relief. Nothing new broken.

She heard a rustle in some blue elderberry plants. A black bear cub tumbled out. Jolene grinned. A bigger bear followed, rising on her back legs.

Jolene wiggled on her bum back up the hill. "It's okay, Momma."

The black bear charged, stones and dirt flying around her paws. Jolene turned and scrambled on her hands and knees. The hot breath of the bear seared her calves. Adrenaline and terror made her forget her ankle was even broken.

Jolene launched herself into the air. Her stomach dropped as she flew up the hill. *Literally flew.* She gasped as she soared over the underbrush, her belly tickled by branches. She heard, rather than saw, the snap of the jaws closing on the spot her leg was just a moment ago.

Flying? Flying!!

When she reached the top of the hill, she crashed to the ground. The two bears were gone, just a shivering bramble bush in their wake. Jolene's arm was throbbing from Kaleisha's bite.

Was it possible she had been given some fairy magic? Standing up on her good leg she pushed off. Cheeks flushed, eyes sparkling, Jolene flew through the forest and back home. She laughed and tried to control her dizzying speed. Adrenaline, joy and disbelief buzzed in her brain. Her path was more like a drunk bee than a soaring eagle, so she kept herself only three feet above the trail.

At home, she limped to the tree she'd originally fallen out of, trying to make a viral video. She climbed to an upper branch and jumped. Instead of plummeting to the ground, she did a strange jerky dance in the air until she landed softly on one foot.

She floated into the house and stationed herself on the couch. Her stomach roiled, and her brain was so busy, she begged off dinner when her parents came home. After everyone went to bed, she practiced floating in her room, adrenaline making sleep impossible.

Jolene jumped when there was a rap at the window.

Kaleisha was hitting the glass with her tiny fists. Jolene let her in.

Kaleisha's wings drooped dejectedly. "I'm finding it hard to fly. Less power in me wings. I must'a given you some of me magic through that dumb bite."

Jolene did a little air spin by her dresser. "And I'm loving it!"

Kaleisha plopped down on the bed. "Give it back!"

"How?"

A fat tear rolled down the fairy's face. "Don't know."

Jolene rubbed between her shoulder blades. "I think I know what might make you feel better."

Jolene put one finger to her lips and lead Kaliesha down the basement. The room was dominated by a massive replica of a condo project. The metal and glass structure stood eight-feet-high with miniature trees, grass, and benches.

Kaleisha gasped in delight.

Jolene smiled at her. "This is one of my mom's prototypes. This replica has a furnished suite, complete with electricity and running water."

Kaleisha's wings threw glitter. "My own condo?"

"Yes, of course!"

Jolene plugged in the replica and the entire building lit up. Sappy elevator music drifted from the lobby. Kaliesha flew into the penthouse and touched the little chairs, lamps, and appliances.

Giggling, she sat on the mini couch, pumping her wee legs. "The only thing that would make this betta is a burrito and Bob Marley."

Jolene winked. "Would a Cheesy Gordita Crunch do?"

"Would it!!!" Kaleisha said.

Jolene poked a music player and the Reggae throbbed out of the lobby speakers. The fairy danced a slow groove, her face glowing.

"Give me one moment." Jolene went upstairs and took out a bit of leftover double-layered beef taco from the fridge. She microwaved it on a bit of paper towel, adding one tortilla chip.

She flew back to the basement, and arranged the food on a mini-plate.

"Kaleisha, dinner is served!"

The fairy sat down at the table, devoured her Cheesy Gordita Crunch, and belched. "You've made me dreams come true. This is the heaven."

"When you get tired of flower nectar, come here and I'll set you up for a night in the condo. Good meal included. In exchange, you teach me how to master this flying thing."

Kaleisha spit out a bit of tortilla. "You got it sister. Time for me to jet."

They returned to her bedroom and Jolene opened her window.

She paled. "I don't know if I'm hallucinating, but are there fifty of your relatives in my yard?"

Kaleisha hid behind the curtain. "Just when I had something good going."

Jolene blinked, her brain trying to catalogue all the mythical visitors. There were Brownies, Leprechauns, Dwarves, Elves, Pixies, and Goblins.

A golden elf with grey eyes approached. "I am Adorellan, elected head of The Fey. Kaleisha, I know you're in there! It has come to my attention you bit a human and bestowed the power of flight upon her."

Kaleisha flew into his face. "I've dealt with it."

An angry murmuring escalated from the assembled group. The Fey came in all colours and sizes, from chubby dark gnomes to iridescent little pixies.

Adorellan grabbed Jolene and screamed, "It is strictly forbidden!" He hauled the shocked girl out the window.

Jolene struggled, but the elf was strong. "I won't tell anyone, I won't fly! I won't--"

"Silence human girl!" The elf's alabaster skin glowed red.

Kaleisha punched Adorellan in the cheek. "This human be my friend! You'll not be hurting her."

Adorellan knocked the fairy into the mob, disappearing under waving arms.

Jolene kicked harder, but even her hefty cast didn't faze the elf.

"It is against our laws," a squat dwarf said.

"It threatens all of us," a group of pixies tittered.

Adorellan raised Jolene up by her collar. "This is the first human ever bitten by a fairy. If she were to receive multiple bites, would she become fully Fey?"

The angry mumbling took on a curious tone and the mob crowded around Jolene. She tried to scream but fear made her mouth so dry she could only squeak. Her eyes searched the crowd, hoping to find her friend. Terror battled disbelief. She was glad she hadn't eaten dinner, not even a bite of the old Taco Bell. If she had, she'd be puking.

Kaliesha kicked a gnome in the ear and fluttered above Jolene's head. "She might turn into a fairy, or she might end up dead!"

Jolene watched Adorellan shrug. "We're going to find out.

Jolene shut her eyes tight as the first dwarf bit her thigh...

The End

11

ABOUT "THE WRITING RETREAT"

~

First published: June, 2020
Strangely Funny VII

THE INSPIRATION for this story came from a writing retreat held on Pelee Island, which is the southernmost point of Canada. How would a horror writer handle a zombie apocalypse?

12

———————

THE WRITING RETREAT

BY ANGELIQUE FAWNS

*L*orelai threw her printed manuscript into the bonfire and watched as the pages curled and smouldered. A little smile played on her lips. She warmed her hands over the fire and hoped a stray ember didn't light up her frizzy dry hair. Being a bleached blonde came with a cost. The other writers at the week-long retreat had already gone back inside. Mosquitos gnawed at her bare legs as a June bug dive bombed her ear.

The four of them had arrived almost a week ago, taking the ferry across Lake Erie from Leamington. Elda, the owner/organizer of the retreat picked them up in a minivan for the fifteen-minute drive to her lakeside home. The idea was to have very little distractions and plenty of quiet writing time. There was no television, no radios and no landline phone. The renowned Canadian author Anabel Boucher was also up for the week to lead workshops. Her novels had won multiple awards detailing fictionalized accounts of missing women in Northern Ontario.

At the beginning of May, the small island was almost deserted because cottagers and day trippers didn't start visiting until the long weekend at the end of the month. Being the southern-most point in

57

Ontario, the trees were already in bloom and an Alfred Hitchcock-ian amount of birds squawked and filled the blue sky.

Lorelai watched the flames dying in the fire pit, and took a deep breath. Her stomach roiled thinking about her creative direction and writing career. At the workshop yesterday, the other writers joked how the worst novels were about definitely zombie stories.

Anabel advised, "No one is looking to publish that sort of story right now. Focus on creating work your readers can connect to. Readers respond to truth."

In fact, this group disparaged any genre literature. Lorelai decided not to share that she'd spent the last year writing a guide on how to survive a zombie apocalypse.

Taking the last swallow of her local Pelee Island Chardonnay, she walked back into the cottage. The décor was rustic and comfortable, lots of heavy wood accenting the interior and a big wood stove warming the rooms. Her fellow writers sat on the couch in the living room with Elda and Anabel. Each had a drink in their hands passionately discussing plot points and levels of vulnerability.

Jennifer was the youngest of the group and pretty in a heroin-chic kind of way. She was working on a fiction book based on the use of psychedelics to treat victims suffering from post-traumatic stress disorder. Jack was an older man with a wide girth and even wider smile. He was writing something called "Swimming in International Waters" about money markets. Tammy was sixty-something, yoga-thin and creating a vegan cookbook. Elda wasn't a writer herself but loved painting pictures of hibernating local species which she sold in the Island gift shop.

Plopping into an antique rocking chair, Lorelai tried to check Facebook –cat memes always cheered her up -but it wouldn't load. Sure enough there were no bars on her cell phone. The house Wi-Fi wasn't working either.

"This might be taking no distractions too far. Check your phones, would you? I can't get Wi-Fi or reception," she asked the others.

Jennifer offered Lorelai the joint she was holding with the tips of her long purple nails.

"Smoking a bit of this might make you not care."

Lorelai politely declined.

"The reception is spotty here, but I like feeling of disconnection," Elda said heading over to the study, "but the green light is on so the router is working."

Jack and Tammy confirmed their phones weren't picking up.

"If we've lost cell service because of aliens, I want to be the first one to get a tour of the ship. I better get some sleep," yawned Jack.

Before he could maneuver out of the deep couch, the lights went out. A collective gasp.

"One minute everyone, don't panic, darkness is wonderful for discovering our true inner selves," Elda stumbled into the kitchen where multiple drawers slammed open and shut.

"Here we go! My emergency drawer with flashlights. Always be prepared. Now we can discover ourselves without tripping" she said passing out mini flashlights.

Lorelai walked to the back-porch windows where the bonfire was still smouldering. Lake Erie lapped gently. It was a gorgeous clear night. Luckily there was full moon illuminating the sky and keeping them out of pure darkness.

"There's no storm or even any clouds in the sky. Why would the electricity go out? Odd."

Elda stood behind her, "Everyone got a flashlight, except Anabel. She must have slipped back to her room."

The air was cool and crisp and Lorelai took a deep breath as she followed Elda down the stone path leading from the cottage to the water's edge.

The guest writing instructor was staying in Elda's small boat house on the shoreline. Luckily it had a pull-out couch, small bathroom and mini kitchen instead of actual boats in it. Elda knocked on the door. No answer. She knocked again then pushed open the door and confirmed it was empty.

"She's not in the living room, and she's not in her boathouse. Perhaps she is using this opportunity to meditate and search for inspiration for her next book," Elda said.

Lorelai walked in and pushed open the bathroom door. Also, empty.

They walked back into the house where the three other writers were amusing themselves telling ghost stories with flashlights under their chins.

"Has anyone seen Anabel?" Lorelai asked.

"She wasn't at dinner today, I had all the lentil soup to myself, as a fellow vegan we have been sharing the meat-less options," Tammy said.

Jennifer was rolling a marijuana cigarette, "I didn't notice she was missing, but it's not like I'm counting heads."

"Maybe she's hooked up with someone. I don't think she goes for nice older guys like me. I bet she is out with a burly workman helping him with his tools," Jack speculated.

"There is nothing we can do about it right now in the dark with no power or cell service, let's go to bed and Anabel will probably turn up in the morning," Lorelai said heading up to her bedroom.

She gave her hair a quick brush, and splashed her face with cold water. Having a pudgy face and curvy figure made her look younger than her thirty years. The loss of electricity and missing writing instructor had distracted her from her writing crisis. She shouldn't panic, there was still time to launch her writing career. Tammy hadn't started writing till she was fifty and was on her third book. Maybe she could figure out a serious literary idea for a novel in her sleep.

The sun woke her up, and she could hear her fellow writers in the kitchen downstairs. Pulling a sweater on against the chill in the still power-less house, she navigated the stairs and joined the grumbling group.

"Somebody should get Elda up. There's no coffee!" Jennifer said, her blue hair spikes lying flat and disorganized against her head. Tammy and Jack nodded in miserable agreement.

Lorelai looked over at the wood stove where last night's fire was cold ash. She went back upstairs and knocked on Elda's door.

"Elda, are you in there?"

The hostess was normally the first one up, spryly getting the coffee going and toasting bread. Lorelai opened the door and saw Anabel standing beside the bed with Elda still sleeping under the sheets. The writing instructor's hair was wild, her face blood-streaked, and her eyes vacant.

"Anabel! Are you okay?" Lorelai stuttered.

Anabel didn't answer and picked up Elda's arm and took a bite out of it. When the sheet shifted, it was obvious this wasn't her first nibble. The hostess was dead.

Lorelai clamped a hand over her mouth to prevent a scream. Was she actually witnessing a real life zombie eating the hostess? Hyperventilating and face flushed from adrenaline, she closed the door quietly. She'd spent a year researching this. Don't panic and don't draw attention to yourself. Remove yourself from the scene. Get help.

In her novel, there were resources for her survivors fighting the undead in the city. This was an almost deserted Island and right now there were no phones. No internet. No power. Plus one zombie cannibal. She didn't like how this equation was adding up. Where did Anabel go last night? Was she actually a zombie or just feeling a little low on iron? Either way, Lorelai was not attending the workshop planned for this afternoon. Spending a minute calming herself down, the wisest course seemed not to panic the others. She quickly ran down the stairs and sat at the breakfast table with Jack and Jennifer.

"Looks like Elda wants to sleep in," she said casually.

Could they tell she was in a living nightmare? They were both eating cold bread with Nutella and didn't seem to notice that she was sweaty and trying to act calm.

"Jack, didn't you tell me that your cell phone picked up the American towers when you were hiking on Fish Point?" Lorelai asked.

"Yes, I was furious when I saw the roaming fee warning yesterday." Jack said.

Jennifer sipped some of yesterday's cold coffee, "I checked Anabel's boat house, and she's still gone."

"If she is in the arms of a burly hunk, why would she hurry home?" Jack laughed.

Lorelai wanted to distract them from any discussion about Anabel.

"I've always wanted to visit the Southern-most point of Ontario. Let's go see if we can piggyback cell service on the Americans," Lorelai said.

It was best to get everyone out of the house before the writing instructor wandered downstairs looking for more breakfast.

She didn't want to panic, but obviously finding help and getting off this accursed island was priority number one. This scene was suspiciously like some of the pages she had thrown into the flames. Then she noticed there were only two at the table.

"Where's Tammy?"

"Oh, she went to do her morning walk," Jennifer said.

Lorelai considered waiting for the older lady but haste was prudent. Grabbing sweaters and hats, they climbed into Elda's mini-van. The keys were in the ignition –hard to steal a car on such a small island. Driving down the dirt road, Lorelai saw Tammy sitting by the side of the road. She slowed down to pick her up, but noticed Tammy was chewing on one of the large brown rabbits that hopped everywhere. Keep driving. Luckily Jennifer and Jack were in the back seat hunched over their cell phones still looking for service. Lorelai tried to slow her breathing. Hysterically she thought, how's Tammy going to fit that into her vegan recipe book? Rare Road Kill Rabbit? She just had to think of this as research. Maybe her zombie survival novel hadn't been such a dumb idea. Might even be a Best Seller.

Fish Point National Park wasn't far and they climbed out of the van. The path was clearly marked with a sign so they walked into the forest on the wood chips lined with white and red trilliums. There were hundreds of birds chirping in the trees. Red-Winged Black birds, Blue-Winged Teals, and Scarlet Tanagers were just a few of the noise makers.

Finally breaking through the woods onto the long stretch of sandy beach, they pulled out their cell phones. The sand came to a long narrow jut, and thirty some odd seagulls scrambled and splashed into the lake as they walked to the furthest point. After a few minutes they looked at each other in dismay. Nothing. No bars.

"Hey, there is someone further down the beach!" Jennifer said.

"I don't like that weird shambling walk. Stay away from him Jen," Lorelai cautioned.

"Look, we all have PTSD of some sort. That guy probably just needs a hit of acid and a therapist. Besides he might have a working phone." Jennifer threw over her shoulder, quickly trotting off.

"Jen, No!" Lorelai hollered, but it was too late, Jennifer was on a mission.

Lorelai started after her, but then Jack distracted her. He was leaning on an old willow tree that twisted out over the lake.

"I wonder if I could get American service if I could get further out on the water. I can see the US Kelley Island from here," Jack said tucking his cell phone into a back pocket and clambering out on the deadwood.

"I'm not sure that's such a wise idea, Jack! It might not hold your weight...." Lorelai warned.

He was several meters out when the branch broke with a loud crack and Jack tumbled into the foamy capped waves.

"I can't swim," he yelled as his bald head bobbed up and under the waves.

Lorelai knew the water was freezing this time of year and she wasn't a strong swimmer. Trying to save Jack would be a suicide mission. Both her writing companions were in jeopardy, this was not how to survive! Stay together, don't do anything dumb. In the last few seconds they had broken both rules. She peered down the beach and saw Tammy fall down as the shambling man jumped on her. A high-pitched scream came as Tammy tried to fight, but was quickly silenced as... Lorelai couldn't watch. She looked around desperately for a branch or something to extend to Jack, but his head had already sunk beneath the water. He didn't come back up again.

Lorelai sobbed, "I can't even," as she desperately tried to dial 911 on her cell.

Of course, no service. Calm down, remember those that panic

end up dead, or even worse -undead. She had been preparing for this for a year with every page she wrote. She'd researched every zombie novel. Watched every episode of The Walking Dead.

She staggered back down the path, paying no attention to the remarkable wildlife. Maybe this was just on the Island? Maybe whatever virus was causing this could be contained? Time to get the first ferry back to the mainland. But then the fact that there was no American or Canadian cell service made her very nervous. And why was there no power? What if Pelee Island was the last place to be affected?

She hopped back into the minivan and drove to the other side of the island to the ferry dock, but the chain link fence was closed. A sign was tacked to the drive-through window.

"Ferry is cancelled until further notice."

A sinking feeling in her gut. This might mean the worst. She parked her car and looked around for someone. Anyone not shambling with a dead-eye stare that is. There was one guy, a fisherman floating in his boat a few feet off shore. Lorelai walked out on a tourist sight-seeing dock so she was almost beside him.

"Excuse me sir, why is the ferry cancelled?"

"No idea. But haven't seen one all day, and my neighbours have become not so neighbourly" he said out of the corner of his mouth around a cigar as he wound fishing line.

"Do you have a landline or cell service?"

"Nope."

"Are there any doctors or police on the island?"

"Not yet."

Lorelai looked at him in frustration, "I am desperate sir. Can you take me to Leamington? I can pay you. My friends are all dead. I need to find out what's going on."

He looked up at her and shifted the cigar to the other side of his mouth. He moved his fishing boat to the dock.

"I figure it's safer on the water than on shore. You don't know what's waiting for you back in the big town, but it may be more of these inhospitable zombie folks. Guess I can't float out here forever. Let's go see if Leamington is still standing."

Lorelai clambered off the dock onto his boat, and sat down on one of the seats at the stern. Several cases of water, a bunch of beef jerky, cucumbers and tomatoes were visible in the cabin. He tossed her a big rain jacket and then turned the boat towards the Canadian mainland.

She patted her pocket where her USB memory stick sat safely. She still had her novel saved digitally. The burning of the paper copy had been symbolic. Her story on how to survive a zombie apocalypse might become very relevant. If there was still a New York Times Best Seller List it may hit the top. As the boat bumped up and down on the waves of Lake Erie, Lorelai tried to think positively. If they got to Leamington and everybody was a zombie, she wouldn't have to go back to work. There would be plenty of time to finish her novel.

13

ABOUT "THE SIREN OF STEM CREEK"

~

*A*n Original Story for Mythical Monsters

CATHERINE WEAVER IS a guest author in this collection, and her murderous story about a siren and a water skeeter is beautifully dark.

CATHERINE WEAVER IS A FOURTH-GENERATION CALIFORNIAN, who believes that the world can be a magical place filled with wonder, especially her native San Francisco Bay Area. She has written award-winning books and stories of fantasy and science fiction set in the area, sparking the imaginations of old and young readers alike.

14

THE SIREN OF STEM CREEK

BY CATHERINE WEAVER

*N*erissa cradled the bloated face of yet another dead lover. His hair floated around her fingers as she gave him a last tender kiss and let his blue-tinged body drift away with the current. A tear spun from her eye into the water of her forest stream--her hallowed refuge, her birthplace, her own soul. Her lovers shouldn't drown in these waters any more than she did.

She blamed the water skeeter.

She broke the surface and fixed him with a steely glare.

"I didn't do nothin'!" He skated away, heading for the reeds.

"Only the guilty are so quick to defend themselves, Skeeter," Nerissa said.

He skidded to a stop and turned, then bobbed up and down on his two-inch-long legs. "Maybe my magic air bubbles can't take the workout you put them through down there." He laughed suggestively.

Nerissa stepped onto the bank. The water rushing down her body solidified into a glimmering gray dress, and she tossed her brown hair dry. Greenish-gray clips that matched her hazel eyes held her hair in place.

She gazed at her lover's tunic and britches on the bank. "You said you'd perfected the process. It was fool proof, you said."

She gathered up the clothes and carried them to the cairn near the old pine. The rock's cry echoed through her clearing when she scraped it aside. She dropped the bundle on top of the others in the hole, then slid the rock back.

Skeeter's tinny voice floated to her from the water. "Well, maybe not proof from *all* fools."

"Stop it, Skeeter!" Nerissa clenched her jaw. She knew she was a fool. Her curse made her one. She had to break it before she went insane.

She paced around her clearing and almost ran into a wooden sign at the path: *Stem Creek. Warning: Deathly Peril to All Who Enter!*

She yanked on it with both hands until it pulled free, sending clumps of dirt and grass flying. Then she threw it into the underbrush. "I need a man to survive my waters, Skeeter. I'll never break my curse like this. You don't want it to work, do you? I'm tempted to call a fish to eat you."

He bobbed anxiously on the water. "No! Give me one more chance!"

She kneeled on the bank and glared at him. "Not many more men will walk down that forest path now that so many have died."

"The next guy'll live. You can bet on it!" He skated over to her.

"You're betting your life on it, Skeeter. I can't lose another one." Nerissa rose and walked to the trail, her song rising in her throat.

What else could she do? Her song had power, but she didn't know how to make a man survive underwater. But Skeeter did.

She'd seen the prototypes: Squirrels lying peacefully underwater encased in Skeeter's bubble, their chests moving quietly up and down.

Something thrashed downstream, pulling her from her thoughts.

She moved to the disturbance and found Skeeter reigning over an ecstasy of destruction. Flies swarmed around her dead lover in the reeds. Fish bites jostled his body. Crows feasting on his head flapped their wings for balance.

Skeeter moved through it all, dodging the fish and sucking on flies.

"Skeeter!"

He tossed a gruesome carcass aside and scooted across to her. "You got a new one already?"

"You *are* doing this on purpose!" Her head pounded. It was all making sense, and she was ashamed. Ashamed of how she'd allowed her desire to cloud her perceptions. Skeeter wasn't some innocent bug who made mistakes—he'd been manipulating her!

"It's not how it looks, Nerissa. Come on, you can't let this bounteous feast go to waste. Have a heart!"

"You're the one with no heart, Skeeter. That man, whatever his name was, might have been the one that broke my curse. I'm on to you now. It's always been your plan to create a new corpse with each attempt. Well, if the next one dies, so do you!"

She dove into the water, her dress melting into the stream, and gave the man a shove downstream, dislodging birds, fish, and bugs.

She glared at Skeeter who cringed in the reeds. "Now that I know what you're doing, I'm going to find a man, and everything will work perfectly this time. Or else."

Nerissa emerged from the water and stood at the trail.

This one would work. She cast her song into the woods. He'd be here soon.

HE WAS different from the others when he wandered into the glade. Instead of a bow slung over his shoulders, he had a lute. His eyes, though glazed by her song, held a brightness beneath his dark eyelashes, and the lines of his face were worn into a permanent look of amusement around his two-day-old beard.

She loved him, of course. She loved them all. But, if possible, she loved him more, in a way that went beyond her curse. This love would last, she knew it. If she could just make sure he lived.

She broke the flow of her song to call, "Skeeter! Get ready!"

The man startled and shook his head. Then he looked questioningly into her eyes and opened his mouth to speak.

She put a finger over his lips and sung to him in almost a whisper until his mouth drifted closed and he brought a hand to her waist. She lifted his bag and lute from his shoulders, and lowered him to the ground, where she helped him pile his clothes and boots neatly by her stream.

They embraced and rolled to the bank. Skeeter was there with his membrane of water held together with surface tension. It enclosed a precious bubble of air. Nerissa watched Skeeter carefully as he brought the bubble closer. She kissed her lover again, ducked them both under the water, and brought their heads up within the captured air. Skeeter flitted around their shoulders, securing the bottom, then raised one leg in a salute.

Nerissa lowered her lover into the water, kissing and humming and wrapping her arms around him, abandoning herself to the power of her curse and her love.

When he returned her kiss, his lips were stronger and more alive than she'd felt before. The scratch of his beard on her chin brought her out of her trance. She opened her eyes, though she hadn't realized she'd closed them. Then she saw it.

The bubble shrank inward with each breath the man took. It plastered itself to his head and cheeks. On the next breath it would be empty.

She had to do something. The only power she had was her song. Could she shape it to some other use?

She changed her tune to one of opening, of expanse, and of air. Yes—there it was—a flutter in the bubble. It grew, to a space of two inches around the man's head.

But her new song had another effect. It was no longer a song of enchantment and being lost in a lover's embrace. The man put two strong hands against her shoulders and pushed her away. Then he kicked hard at the water and shot to the surface.

She followed, knocking Skeeter aside when her head emerged.

The fool had stayed right above them, waiting. He'd just used up her last scrap of trust in him. He was beyond redemption.

She couldn't let that mean her own lost redemption too.

Her lover was already on the shore, scrambling for his clothes.

She jumped out of the water and landed on him, clinging to his shoulders. "Please! Please stay, my love. I won't harm you, I promise. I need you!" Hot tears stung her cheeks.

He ignored her cries and pulled on his clothes. In desperation, she sucked in a breath and sang.

The man threw her off him and stuffed grass in his ears. "I can't believe I succumbed to your spell! I, Jack Thorn, the bane of all women, fell to the Siren of Stem Creek! I almost deserved to die—but not quite!" With those last words he swept to his feet, fully clothed, and drew his lute across his chest.

Then he sang the sweetest song Nerissa had ever heard, accompanying himself with desultory plucks of the lute. She relaxed onto the bank, wondering what she'd been so worried about. There was nothing here but the rippling stream, fragrant grasses, and this lovely man with a rope around her throat.

She shot bolt upright and wedged a hand between her neck and the rope. She threw the rope to the ground as she rose to her feet, leaning over him. She tore the grass from his ears. "How dare you? I love you!"

"You love me to death, you mean. You almost killed me!" He stood and leaned down to glare straight into her eyes.

Heat rose up her neck into her cheeks and ears. His scent filled her head. She fought back the urge to sing, and forced out common speech. "You almost killed *me*!"

Skeeter's surprisingly clear voice interrupted them from the surface of the stream. "Now, now, don't you think it's time you love-bugs got back in the water? Come on, siren, where's your song?"

She was so shocked by his tone that she turned to answer him.

A rush of grass against boots, and the man was across the glade, headed for the trees. She couldn't let him leave! He was her last chance!

She sprang through the air and landed on him, wrapping her arms around his chest, and dragging him to the ground just under the first tree's branches.

"Please help me," she whispered in his ear, not trusting herself to not sing if she gave her words voice. "I promise not to sing."

"Get off me! You're death!" He rolled to his hands and knees.

She clung to his back, weighing him down, but she knew she only had seconds before he threw her off. "*I'm* not death. It's my curse. You and I together can break it!"

He did throw her off, but instead of running down the trail, he turned and looked down at her. "What do you mean?"

"I'm the spirit of Stem Creek, and my life is bound to this water. I grew lonely one day and sang to the Rain my mother, asking for a companion. She sent a human man in answer, and I took him into my deep water bed, but he drowned. I was wracked with grief, but soon a compulsion came over me to sing until another man came.

"This cycle has repeated without my will. Skeeter showed me a bubble he created to provide air so the man can live, but he made sure it would fail every time. But just now, I made it work for you using my song. You have the magic of song too, so I feel certain if we sing together, you will live and I'll no longer have the compulsion to bring another man to me with song."

He shook his head, "I don't know why I'd risk my life for you. I've got places to go, people to see."

She wrapped her arms around him. "But I love you! You must be the one for me, the man my mother the Rain has sent me. Don't you feel anything for me?"

"I'm flattered, I can say that much. You're beautiful and magical and I alone have resisted your song, but I intend to keep it that way."

He turned on his heel and her heart rose to her throat with desperation. She called out, "So you're afraid you can't do it?"

He stopped walking, keeping his back to her.

"I thought you were a master at your music, but if you don't even believe it yourself, it must not be true."

He turned back to her, his voice harsh. "All right, all right, I'll do it. If I don't, I'll spend the rest of my life wondering if I would have succeeded."

With glad heart, she took his hand and burst into song. The repressed tune exploded from her lips. Jack sang with her, in harmony, complementing every note.

Between phrases, she called, "Skeeter, ready an air bubble now, and you may be redeemed!"

"Will I, Mistress? Will I, really?" There was that edge in Skeeter's voice again.

She and Jack stepped to the water's edge, but no air bubble awaited them. Instead, Skeeter stood on the water at the vanguard of a phalanx of decay.

Rotted bodies of former lovers whom she thought had long since made their way to the cleansing sea, wrapped in decomposing reeds and dead fish were surrounded by bugs of every kind. The buzzing of the swarms drowned out Nerissa and Jack's song, and the rising stench made her gag.

Jack's voice was replaced by the sound of him emptying his stomach in a bush behind her. She squeezed his hand, willing him not to run.

"Skeeter! What is this?" Her voice was no longer a song, but a wail.

He scooted closer to the bank. "Riches, my dear naiad. Riches! Stop trying to cut me off and be a good girl and bring this next one to his watery grave, would you?"

"Never!" She raised her voice in defiance, bringing the full force of her magic down on the water skeeter.

Birds dove from the sky with open beaks, swallowing bugs as they came, but none touched Skeeter. They swooped back to the sky, and circled above.

Nerissa sang even harder, and fish leaped from the stream, catching water skeeters in their mouths, but not Skeeter.

He advanced across the narrow span of water to stand on the water lapping at Nerissa's feet. "You're cursed, and do you know who cursed you?" He bobbed on his bent knees. "Yes, I see you do. It was me. I couldn't have my breadbasket leaving, now could I?"

Nerissa sank to her knees and turned to Jack. He wiped the back of his hand across his mouth and looked at her with disgust. "You're a monster." He stood and turned his back to her.

The compulsion to bring him to her overtook her. She clamped her mouth shut but the song within crawled up her throat, wrenching at her vocal chords, tearing at her tongue.

Before it burst from her mouth, she lurched at Jack, grabbing him around the knees. When he turned to kick at her face, she caught his eye and pleaded with him, gesturing him to open his mouth.

Silently she prayed to her mother the Rain that Jack would understand before the enchanted song flew from between her teeth and escaped into the air.

Jack's eyes glazed over, his jaw went slack. He fumbled at his shirt's buttons. He hadn't understood. He was just more bug food. Even while she continued to sing, she bowed her head at his feet.

A tear dropped onto a toe. She watched its trail as it meandered around the bone and disappeared into the space between toes.

Then a hand grasped her arm and lifted her up. She gazed into Jack's bright, no longer glazed eyes. He nodded and opened his mouth. His song hit her like a buck with lowered antlers. She fell back, but his hand around her arm steadied her. She felt his song blasting something from her, something she hadn't realized was there. Something dark and slimy twisted from her. She could see it wrapped around the notes of her own hallowed song.

She changed her song to push the evil threads from it, and saw them unraveling.

"No!" Skeeter jumped into the air and landed on her back.

His feet tapped out a rhythm, and the dark thread responded, wrapping itself more tightly around her song. She tried to shake him off, but when she moved, her feet echoed the water skeeter's rhythm on her skin. Her own tune grew darker, twisting Jack's with it.

As he bent to kiss her, the foul corpses washed onto the bank, their stench rising up to engulf her and Jack.

She desperately wanted to feel the touch of those lips, but knew if she gave in, it would mean another death on her hands. Why had the Rain cursed her so?

Wait. Her mother hadn't cursed her—that was Skeeter and whatever spirit of decay had given him power. The Rain had only ever given her blessing. She'd given Nerissa life, and consecrated her hallowed stream.

She turned her lips so they brushed Jack's cheek and not his mouth, and with all her will, sang to her mother the Rain.

First it was just a murmur, but Jack caught her song, and altered his tune a bit to join hers. Skeeter's tapping on her back was out of sync, so she concentrated on her own rhythm, and made her toes tap to her own song. Soon she and Jack were swaying to their song, ignoring the incessant drumming of Skeeter's feet.

Their song became a waltz and they danced across the small glade.

Plop!

A drop of rain landed on her head.

"No!" Skeeter screamed. "Stop that!"

Plop! Plop!

Nerissa raised her voice now with more confidence, and Jack held her more firmly.

Plop! Plop! Plop!

The drops became a downpour. Jack's eyes met Nerissa's, full of fire and defiance. Together they danced through the rain as it dislodged the stinking mass of death from the bank and washed it away down past the reeds and toward the sea.

"Mistress, please, stop! I can't stay on while you're dancing like that!" Skeeter's feet were no longer transmitting any sense of rhythm, but were instead scrabbling for purchase.

Nerissa gripped Jack harder, and focused on their song, splashing their *one-two-three* in the muddy glade.

"Noooo!" Skeeter gave a final cry as he was caught in the water sluicing down Nerissa's back and carried to the ground to be trampled underfoot.

Nerissa's cheeks tightened in a fierce grin. She and Jack whooped the final note of their song and threw themselves together with a crash.

Their kiss was wild and unbridled, their bright eyes wide open, and laughter escaped the sides of their mouths. There was no trace of a trance, no dream-like quality.

The clouds broke, easing the rain to a light mist that refracted the light of her glade into a rainbow.

Nerissa handed Jack his boots and he slipped them on. Then he slung his lute over his back, grabbed his pack, and held his hand out to her. "Want to get out of here?"

She shook her head sadly. She could never leave her glade. Then the rainbow caught her eye. The Rain's sign to her that her curse was broken glowed in the mist on the trail. She could leave whenever she liked.

Her heart fluttered in her breast like a young bird as she took Jack's hand and followed the rainbow out of her glade.

15

———

ABOUT "WYATT & THE WHOG"

∾

First published: June 2020
Mansion Press — Little Boy Lost

In this adventure we meet slave master Whogs who trap and imprison hapless children.

16

WYATT AND THE WHOG

BY ANGELIQUE FAWNS

yatt had found the most amazing thing that morning, and he can hardly wait to take a closer look. The lump in his pocket keeps distracting him as he spreads the fresh wood chips around the horse stall. He's only twelve, but his dad trusts him to get the morning chores done without supervision. His skinny chest swells with pride at the thought. The smell of pine tickles his nostrils as he looks down the dirty barn aisle. One stall down, five more to go.

"A diamond is merely a lump of coal that did well under pressure," his dad liked to chortle.

Wyatt didn't exactly know what that meant, but during his summer school break it translated into him shoveling racehorse poop for an hour every morning. He knows he should finish the stalls first, but the wiggling bulge keeps distracting him. Tossing his shaving fork into the wheelbarrow, he climbs up onto the stack of small square hay bales at the end of the aisle.

Reaching into the pocket of his overalls, he pulls out the large lumpy toad he'd found behind the barn that morning. Setting it down on the top of the highest alfalfa bale, he stares into its bulbous eyes. It's the largest Fowler's toad he's ever seen, as big as his palm with green-grey skin and a white stripe. He's running his fingers along the knobby black bumps on its back when it leaps into the air and clear off the haystack, soaring like a mini-meteor into the stall of his dad's prize racehorse.

The toad lands with a thump, square on the mare's back. With a startled snort, the horse bucks and charges around her stall trying to dislodge the unknown assailant. The green amphibian tumbles into the straw and hops safely into a corner. Kicking down the wooden door with her hind feet, the horse spins with the speed that makes her the stable's top earner, bolting away down the aisle.

It's *not* the toad's fault that Wyatt had left the barn door open. That's Wyatt's fault. Everyone knew you shut the barn door. Always. But this one time, excited by the specimen he had squiggling in his pocket, Wyatt had left it open. And of course, the mare beelines for it.

Wyatt scrambles off the hay, running after her hoping she doesn't head towards the busy regional road. The mare, aptly named "Rollin in Dough", is galloping towards the cow paddock.

This could have been a good thing if she had been stopped by the three-post cedar rail fence. But Rollin doesn't even slow as she crashes through. She continues her charge, coming to an abrupt stop in front of the herd of ten wide-eyed cows.

The heifers and a few steers had been contentedly munching on the early summer grass, but this unexpected intrusion causes widespread panic. Wyatt loved cows; he especially loved hopping up on one of the steers and holding on for as many seconds as he could before being bucked off. But he knew they didn't always run the most logical way. The startled cows stampede and surge towards, rather than away, from Rollin. The bewildered horse spins around and gallops back out of the paddock with ten panic-stricken cows following.

The whole herd of them run directly into the newly sprouting soybean crop. Wyatt watches in horror as they make big sweeping circles trampling the plants. He had helped his dad plant the thirty-acre field, and it had taken a whole day.

Of course, this is when his dad pulls into the driveway to watch his three streams of income either being destroyed—or doing the destroying. The cows are frenziedly tearing around while Rollin stands quivering at the side of the field.

"What in tarnation! Wyatt, go saddle up two horses, we've got to round these blasted cattle up!" his dad bellows, hopping out of his pickup truck.

"Sorry, Dad, I'm on it, sir!"

Wyatt hustles to the barn, cringing at the dirty stalls and quickly throwing saddles on two of the retired racehorses. His dad charges in after him and they both mount up and gallop out into the field. If he wasn't so frightened of his dad's rage, Wyatt would have enjoyed herding the cattle like a real cowboy back into their pasture. The sweaty horses dodge and dance as they work, and Wyatt stays on like a pro.

Once all the cows trot back, exhausted from their big adventure, Wyatt guards the hole in the fence as his dad quickly pounds up some new rails. They put the horses back into their stalls, and his dad glares at him as he grabs a lead shank and goes out to bring Rollin back in. After watching the action, she had started munching on some grass under a tree and was in no danger of going further.

"Pretty girl, what did you do to your legs?"

His dad ignores Wyatt as he tends to the bloody wounds on Rollin's legs from knocking over the cattle fence. Rollin is now going to be off her race schedule for a couple months to heal.

Then he turns to his son and muttered ominously, "Just... go... for... a *big long walk*!"

Wyatt quickly goes into Rollin's stall and puts the toad back into his pocket before he hightails it to the forest at the back of the property. He walks alongside the river roaring with extra water from the spring melt. The path is on a sandy cliff rising perhaps twenty feet above the bubbling depths. Kneeling down, he takes out the toad and lets it hop into the bushes.

Wyatt notices a big snapping turtle napping a few feet down the bank. He leans forward to see if he can grab it. The sandy edge of the cliff gives way and he tumbles down the embankment. He splashes into the shockingly cold current. Gasping and struggling, he tries to keep his head above water as the current pulls him along. There is a small waterfall approaching and Wyatt tries to backpedal. He slips beneath the surface, able to see the blurry blue sky above him but he couldn't seem to swim in the right direction. Just when he thinks he couldn't hold his breath any longer he feels his feet collide with the riverbed. The sand gives way beneath him as he's pulled into a tunnel. With a massive whoosh, he's sucked a short distance and lands with a thump beneath a tree.

His befuddled brain tries to process the sights in front of him. He's sitting on thick, lush grass more blue than green, and a soft bed of pine-like needles lay under his bum. Did he fall out of the big hole in the tree behind him?

He rubs his arms trying to get his circulation to return and hears a soft noise behind him. Turning to look over his shoulder, his heart almost stops. A big alien looking creature is hopping towards him. It looks like an enormous toad, almost like the one he had just set free, but way bigger with intelligent eyes, floppy ears, and overly long legs.

WALLY IS A WHOG. Right now, he's hunting, his slimy snout sniffing the air, shuffling rapidly across the field. But he's not looking for food. No, he likes to eat those tasty four-winged flies that flit across his lake. Right now, he smells human child.

In his excitement he picks up his pace, his webbed feet flapping through the grass. One has obviously fallen through a portal, and now the race is on.

Wally sees a cloud of purple dust rising up in the distance. His deadly enemies, the Moogs, are galloping towards him. Wally likes to travel solo, but the antelope-like Moogs are always in a herd. They are also looking to collect those that tumble into this world, but each has different plans for the visitor. But Wally doesn't think they are going to get this kid. He may move slower than his long-legged adversaries, but he is much closer to the boy who is beside the big tree that occasionally spits out children from the cavernous hole in its trunk.

The new arrival is sitting on the blue grass under the portal tree. His eyes are wide, and he looks very confused.

What a wonderful specimen! Tall, strong, and ten good fingers. Perfect. As Wally lumbers up, the boy leaps to his feet and backs away. A full-grown Whog weighs around three hundred pounds. With amphibian skin, yellow double lidded eyes, and full body warts it looks like a toad.

Wally must reassure the boy before he runs. The Whog leans forward and swabs his face with a gooey kiss.

"Welcome, guest. Be at rest."

"What kind of crazy toad are you?" the boy stutters.

"Ah. I'm not a toad. I am a Whog. And you are new. It's nice to meet you to. Wally Whog, through and through."

"A Whog, what is a Whog?"

"Well a Whog is a Whog, and Whogs know what they are. Friendly and loves to snog." Wally snuffles with a wet gurgle.

The boy reaches a tentative hand forward and pats Wally's back. "Friendly is good. I love your back bumps."

"What is your name, child? Reciprocal identification is good social presentation."

"I'm Wyatt. Where am I?"

Just then the ground starts to rumble and particles of dust begin to fall on them.

"It's the Moogs! A big herd of them from what I can hear! Quick, climb on my back, buddy," Wally says.

Wyatt asks, "Moogs? What is a Moog?"

"No time, no time, we must go. Or what might happen I cannot know." Wally bends low to the ground.

A few bobbing antlered heads are now visible through the purple haze. Wyatt leaps onto Wally's back like he's been riding Whogs all his life and they start to shamble at his fastest speed towards the brackish lake a few meters away.

The elegant four-legged creatures, maybe twenty of them, arrive at the tree just as Wally leaps into the lake. Frustrated mews reverberate through the air as the Moogs paw up the ground with their hooves.

As Whogs actually build their homes in water, Wally's round body sails easily across the lake. Wyatt clings to his back and even starts whooping and pretending to spin an invisible rope as they glide through the viscous water. After about fifteen minutes of swimming Wally drags them up onto the shore. One side of the lake was flat meadowland, but this side is rocky and is at the base of a mountain range.

Wyatt slides off Wally's back and says, "Thank you! I guess you saved me from something?"

Wally doesn't answer and starts hopping towards the mountainside. Wyatt follows him into a damp tunnel.

"Where are we going? Please, Mr. Wally?"

"A little more, we're almost to the floor." He hops at a good pace down the dimly lit path.

Shortly they emerge onto a ledge that looks out onto an enormous pit of conveyor belts and clanking machinery. Children work with blue stones as Whogs look on with whips held in their goopy mouths.

Wally wraps a webbed paw around Wyatt's wrist before he can try to escape. "No, my fine young man, you cannot run, your new life has begun!"

"But the Moogs?!" Wyatt cries.

"They would have sent you straight home, and you would have missed out on our Boostone Dome."

Wally drags Wyatt down the ramp that leads to the factory floor.

"So, you weren't saving me, you were kidnapping me? For child slave labour?"

"For Whogs to be wealthy, we need children who are healthy."

Wally places him in a line of ten or so children picking up bits of blue stone and rubbing them with big yellow leaves. The conveyor belt cranks along on creaky struts made of broken branches and bits of stump.

Wally shuffles away back up the ramp and out the tunnel. Out to hunt for his next kid. They don't pop through that often, but he has to always be on the lookout!

~

THE BOY CLOSEST TO HIM, who looks about ten, gives him a quick smile and whispers under his breath, "Polishing is the easiest job. If you get the Whogs angry, you're sent to the rock wall to chip out stone. That's the worst job. Next comes loading and unloading carts. You want to be a polisher."

Wyatt grabs a leaf and joins the boy on the assembly line.

"I'm Wyatt. How did you get here?"

"My name is Pierre." He doesn't look up. "I was rock climbing with my dad in a National Park two years ago, when I slipped. I fell into a little crevice that should have landed me in the Diablo River but instead I ended up in a saltwater pond and met Wally."

"I fell into a river by my house and ended up on some blue grass under a tree. Where do all these kids sleep?" asks Wyatt.

"We live in a cave beside the mines. It has cots, a bathroom pit room, and an underground mountain stream we can swim in. They feed us mystery meat sandwiches twice a day. Gross, but better than nothing."

Mystery meat and bathroom pits. Wyatt doesn't mind roughing it, but that does sound gross.

"Do we ever go outside?"

"Nope. Only the rock chippers go outside."

Wyatt thinks for a minute. "You just met me, but can I ask you to trust me? I have a plan to get out of here."

His dad always says, "Thinking will not overcome fear, but action will," and Wyatt has never been known for his patience. He's not hanging around to be a slave to overgrown toads.

"Well, it's been two years. What do I have to lose? Except be sent back to mining duty," says Pierre.

"Exactly!" Wyatt picks up a piece of Boostone and hurls it at the closest Whog.

Pierre's eyes bug out. "What are you doing? Stop!"

"Do it! Toss some Boostone." Wyatt picks up another stone, flinging it at the guard.

The Whog roars in anger as little blue stones bounce off his head.

Pierre bends over to get his own rock, but then two Whogs slither over and grab them.

"You'll pay the fine! Off to the mine," one snarls.

Pierre sobs as they're hauled up a back ramp. "Is this really your plan? To go from the best job to the worst? I wish I'd been on a different part of the line."

Wyatt hisses, "Trust me."

He's blinded briefly by the sunshine as they come out into a valley where kids scrape at the mountain side with rocks and big sharpened sticks. Dull blue spots freckle the stone like spattered paint.

They pick up sticks out of a pile at the end of the row of kids and join the ranks scratching at the wall.

"I trusted you like I trusted the Whog," Pierre groans as he works his stick into the wall.

Wyatt looks around surreptitiously until he sees the closest tree. It looks like an old oak tree, but the leaves are purple and the branches grow in loops.

"Follow my lead just one more time," he whispers to Pierre.

He grabs Pierre's arm, he charges towards the tree, the other boy stumbling behind him. The guard Whogs take a few seconds to figure out what's going on and then roar in anger. Their big bodies don't move terribly quickly, but they lumber after them. Wyatt and Pierre are already at the base of the tree. Wyatt starts climbing up the lower branches with Pierre right behind him. The Whogs lash their whips at their scrambling feet but can't climb themselves with their webbed feet. It takes opposable thumbs to mine Boostone and climb things.

They rest at the very top of the tall purple tree where they are out of reach of the Whogs and their whips. The other kids have stopped working and are cheering and hooting encouragement.

Pierre gasps for breath and yells, "Now what?" over the cacophony of his fellow slaves.

One of the Whogs is at the bottom of the tree staring balefully at them, while the other guards try to quiet the excited children who have completely abandoned their labours. A couple of kids try to run to the tree as well but are grabbed quickly by upset Whogs. In order to contain the chaos, the mining team is shuffled back into the mountain while a couple of guards remain staring up at the escapees.

"Well, I figured the Whogs couldn't climb trees." Wyatt crawls further up his curly wide branch. "Now it's time for us to figure out our next move."

Pierre points at a white creature in the sky approaching them. "Maybe we don't have to!"

"Is that a flying unicorn?" He asks in wonder.

The graceful form approaching them glistens in the sunshine as its iridescent wings make a whooshing sound. The big powerful wings create an air current that stirs Wyatt and Pierre's hair as it alights on one of the stronger branches.

"Finally, children smart enough to take to the trees! We can't rescue you from the ground, but we can from the air!" comes a deep, beautiful voice.

"What are you?" asks Wyatt.

"I am a Unicork and my name is Atwan. We don't have much time! Climb aboard and we will get you home." Kind blue eyes dominate the beautiful long face of the creature.

Wyatt and Pierre climb aboard his muscular back and entwine their fingers in the white mane. He launches off the tree branch while the screams of the Guard Whog rise up behind them.

"So, where did the Whog find you? Your way in is also your way home," Atwan rumbles as the big body beneath the boys climbs into the air. Wyatt marvels at the feel of the muscles flexing under his bum; he bets Atwan could win a race or two.

Wyatt and Pierre described their landing places, leaning forward into Atwan's ear. He shifts his flight pattern to Wyatt's tree.

"Our world is called Asalon. A war is raging here. Our currency is Boostone and the Whogs have become wealthy by capturing children who fall through portals and making them slaves. Most of us believe all beings should be free, even lost children, and we battle those who don't. But the Whogs are strong."

Atwan lands beside Wyatt's tree, and he slides off the Unicork's back after giving Pierre a high-five.

"You saved me. I'm glad I trusted you after all," Pierre says.

Wyatt grins at him. "Maybe we can find each other in our world!"

Then he bows to the Unicork. "Thank you so much, Atwan! But what about those other captured kids?"

"Hopefully those on the mining team now know we can collect them from the trees. We will increase our patrols around the Whog mine. But the guards will be more alert now. Is there a way for you to warn the children of your world?" Atwan slowly extends his magnificent wings. "Beware the Whog. Trust the Moog."

As Wyatt prepares to crawl back into the dark opening, he turns. "Yes, I like writing stuff. Maybe I can pen a story that warns of the Whogs and Boo-stone slavery. Maybe I can even make a podcast or something."

Atwan nods regally at him as he takes to the air with Pierre clinging to his back and waving at Wyatt.

Wyatt eases into the tree and the darkness engulfs him as he falls into oblivion.

WYATT AWOKE with the cold water of the river lapping at his feet, soaked and disoriented. Was it a dream? Or did he actually get kidnapped by an enormous toad thing called a Whog and saved by a Unicork? Either way he promised to warn other kids; time to start writing a story. But first on his agenda is the farm chores. He's certainly learned his lesson about getting his work done before play. Plus he's proud of himself. He's proved himself to be a cool customer under pressure, large scary toads with whips, no matter.

He'll finish those stalls and then he'll start writing a story. He'll call it "Wyatt and the Whog."

17

—————

ABOUT "THE ROUGAROU"

~

First published: December 2019
Soteira Press— *The Monsters We Forgot V.3*

THE ROUGAROU IS *a mythical shape-shifter* originating from the folklore of French-speaking communities in Louisiana, particularly Cajun culture.

18

THE ROUGAROU

BY ANGELIQUE FAWNS

My husband Benoit was moving the two of us up north, where the summers are short and the winter creates frostbite patches on your skin. Being originally from Louisiana, my Creole blood didn't like the cold. This was Canadian logging country, in one of the least inhabited areas of Ontario. Grocery shopping was a day trip, and the closest neighbour was an hour's snowmobile ride away.

Our romance started at a big television network in Toronto. I sold commercial airtime and Benoit was the creative lead in the marketing department. More than just our ad campaigns clicked. I was instantly attracted to this burly man with an amazing imagination. We also connected through our French Louisiana roots. His ancestors were run out of Nova Scotia and settled there before migrating back to Quebec, and my descendants came from African slaves brought to work on French colonial plantations. We both loved reading the history and colourful superstitions of our New Orleans culture. We made an odd couple, my petit frame and coffee-coloured skin next to his hulking body and red-headed paleness. He proposed to me by piercing an arrow through a voodoo doll's heart with a ring attached to it.

There was great content on Netflix that featured legends of our people, including some spine-tingling horror movies. Unfortunately, we weren't the only ones who loved Netflix. As more and more TV viewers cut the cord and cancelled their cable subscriptions, conventional television suffered. We were both let go when the company's shares sank to penny stock level. The owners filed for bankruptcy protection, and hundreds of people were walked out the door without severance packages.

My husband had an odd weekend hobby where he liked to drive into the Canadian Shield forests and strap chains to Belgian horses (Belgians are the strongest breed of heavy horse) and skid logs out of forests. Wealthy land owners found it a novelty to hire him for a weekend. It put a few dollars in his pockets and kept him in incredible shape. Environmental horse logging was a dying art but his grandfather had cleared land with draft horses for a living up in the Gatineau region of Quebec, so Ben came by it naturally. When his grandfather died, Ben took the two old horses and boarded them at a stable north of Toronto with big grassy fields. He said working with Betty and Bob the Belgians reminded him of his Acadian roots.

We'd put off starting a family to focus on our careers and now neither of us had one. Toronto was an expensive city, and regular jobs in short supply so I couldn't say no when he found a lucrative job as a logger almost four hours north-east. He was hired to clear trees near Bon Echo Park for a rich family who wanted to open a private campground. Using horses to do the logging made sense to keep the trails and land undamaged.

Part of Benoit's pay was free furnished accommodation on a small acreage with a barn for Betty and Bob, his grandfather's Belgians. We were renting a condo in downtown Toronto, so we broke the lease and sold all our furniture on Kijiji. If I thought that process made me miserable, I had no idea what was in store for me. We packed up his pickup truck with the bare essentials, our large American Bulldog Daisy, and started the long drive north.

I'd thought cottage country was the wilderness. Wrong. Once we got into the County of Frontenac, it was obvious why no one had settled here after the early logging boom. The land was hilly, harsh and truly remote. For the last hour there wasn't a restaurant, store, or even a poutine stand, only a few old lonely shacks here and there.

After what seemed forever, Ben pulled into a two-acre property with an old double-wide trailer on blocks. It backed onto a huge forest so it would be easy for him to hitch up the horses and get to work. But I couldn't see anything else good about it. The house had aluminum siding, a crooked porch, and small windows. Smoke billowed out of the chimney and a pile of logs sat outside. Great. Probably no central heating.

"Ben, you've got to be kidding?" I asked as we turned onto the snow-covered property.

"Hey, it's not that bad! It's only for a year Louisa. Think how much fun you are going to have keeping the fireplace stocked with wood," he gave me a big grin and reached over Daisy's back to give my short black hair a ruffle.

I kept my mouth shut. There was really nothing he could do about it. And I loved him, so I was going to endure this. We unpacked and settled the horses into the small barn. At least the stables were quaint with an old-school hay loft and a wide aisle down the middle. Going back into the trailer-house I turned the tap at the cracked ceramic sink to get a glass of water. It was an odd yellow colour and smelled like sulphur. Good thing we had some bottled water. There wasn't a fireplace, but instead a black wood stove that ate logs voraciously. Mysterious stains marked the walls.

I could get used to the rundown furnishings, well water, and wood stove. What I couldn't get used to was the howling. Every night the eerie serenade of a wolf made my blood run cold.

"Ben, do you hear that?" I asked shaking him awake the first few nights after he crawled into bed exhausted from logging.

"It's just the January winds. They pick up coming down the mountain side," he said giving me a hug and promptly falling back asleep.

Labouring all day in the freezing cold made him sleep like the dead. Benoit got up with the sun and took Betty and Bob out to pull down oak and ash trees. He didn't return till sundown. Then he had to bed down the horses and give them grain and fresh water before coming in himself.

There is nothing quite like the smell of man sweat mixed with horse, manure, and chainsaw oil. Ben would take off his wet boots and hang the insoles by the fire along with his damp pants and jacket. The whole house would be permeated with the foul odour. One more thing I had to learn to tolerate. I didn't sleep well at night and it made me edgy. I was sure the howling was intensifying. That was not the wind. I took comfort from Daisy's big warm body draped over my feet. I'm sure my 140lb bulldog could take on a supersized wolf. Or at least distract it while I ran away.

After about a week of huddling in the house, trying to make it homey, it was time to brave the cold. I hadn't ventured into thigh-high snow yet, but by now Ben and his skidding equipment had made a good trail. Shivering with teeth chattering, I got out of bed and bundled up with sweat pants and three sweaters. There was coffee left in the bottom of the pot, so I poured myself a cup of the now thick sludge and pulled on my boots, snow pants and thick down jacket. The puffy coat along with three sweaters made a scarf redundant. I could hardly turn my neck already doing my imperson-ation of the Stay Puft Marshmallow Man.

Daisy and I headed out the backdoor and started following Ben's footprints to the barn. The real path would start there. The cold made my nostril hairs freeze and my lungs started a long slow burn. When I got to the barn, I pulled open the sliding door and went in to warm up for a minute. The horses truly lived in nicer digs then we did. Climbing the wood rung ladder, I went up to explore the hay loft. There were spiderwebs coating the window at the end. Rubbing a hole in the dirt, I peered out at endless miles of trees up the moun-tain. A gorgeous sight with the sun reflecting off the tips of the Fir and Pine trees. I made a plan to get cross-country skis next time we went to town.

Looking down to the side I saw a big indentation in the hay, like something has been laying there. Bending down for a closer look I saw some rough black and brown hair. Bear, maybe? Picking up a clump, the coarse mass certainly wasn't bear. The thought that it might be the wolf I heard howling made me shiver even in the warm barn under my layers. I noticed the hay still felt warm. Getting up quickly I hustled back to the ladder. Just before my head dropped past the loft floor, I saw two masked black eyes staring at me. An enormous raccoon strolled out from behind a round bale and settled back in her spot. I felt a little ridiculous, what kind of monster was I imagining anyways? Daisy was in the aisle waiting for me. We headed out of the barn, but my unfounded fear had coated me in sweat and I didn't want to catch a worse chill. I abandoned the winter walk idea and decided to tell Ben that we had a raccoon issue when he got home. The creature was probably stealing all our horse grain.

Except he did not come home that evening. Our spicy seafood stew sat untouched in the slow cooker.

Daisy and I waited by the backdoor staring down the trail as the sun sank behind the mountain. I tried to will the sight of the old Belgians and Ben to appear, but nothing happened. Cold terror crept up the back of my spine.

Rather than sit still and let the very last rays of light disappear, I put on all my warm gear again and grabbed an industrial-sized flashlight. This time Daisy and I rushed all the way down the footpath, past the barn, and onto the horses' skidding trail. As soon as we entered the forest, the little bit of light from the sun was obscured. It was really dark. I couldn't tell if the icy chill I was feeling was from the cold or from dread. Walking as fast as I could on the icy trail, I tried not to look into the black trees on either side of me. Daisy scampered eagerly through the undergrowth, her nose guiding her. This was her first real walk off the property.

"Benoit! Are you out here! Ben! Call out if you need help!" I hollered every few feet.

At first, I heard nothing back, but then a long slow howl filled the air. I stopped in my tracks and my heart thudded to an awful full stop. Daisy nudged me and a low growl emanated from her throat. Piercing the night, I heard the eerie howl again and my feet moved me forward before

I became paralyzed with fear. Rushing forward into the black, only the thin light from the flashlight stopped me from tripping over roots.

Up ahead I could see a clearing made by Ben's logging efforts. Charging into the wide-open space, a glow came from the full moon cresting over the trees. Once again, I heard the howl. A big chestnut horse burst out of the trees on the far side and came galloping across the clearing. By the white stripe on her face I could tell it was Betty. She had her hauling collar on but was missing the rest of the harness and chains. She came straight for me but luckily, she slid to a stop before trampling me and I raised a hand to her cheek. Her eyes were wide open with the whites of them showing and sweat coated her body. A froth covered her chest and neck.

"Whoa girl. Where's Benoit?" Where's your partner Bob?" I said as I stroked her neck calmingly.

My eyes quickly assessed her body and I noticed a bit of blood on her side. Uh oh. Before I could take a closer look, the howl started up again, and this time it sounded very close. Betty reared up and galloped down the path towards home.

Now I knew something terrible had happened. Was the team attacked by a wolf pack? Where was Benoit? He would never leave his horses. Up ahead I saw a dark form laying in the snow by the edge of the clearing. Daisy charged ahead of me and started whining with joy. It must be Ben. Running at full tilt, I crashed onto the snow beside him and pushed Daisy back from licking his face.

"It's me, Louisa, are you okay?"

His eyes were open and he stared silently at me.

"What happened? Are you hurt?" I asked while scanning his body for injury.

I couldn't see anything immediately wrong with him until he pointed at his leg. His chainsaw pants were ripped and I could see blood underneath them.

"Did you cut your leg with your chainsaw? Can you walk?" I gasped, trying to get the dwindling glow from the flashlight close enough so I could take a better look.

"I... I didn't cut my leg. I was bitten."

"What? Bitten by what?" I said, trying to fight tears, but keeping my panic under control. I was going to have to get us out of here.

Just then the low howl started up again, and Daisy turned and took off into the trees.

"Daisy! No, Daisy come back!" I screamed into the darkness.

"Let her go Louisa and help me up," Ben grabbed my arm. I tried to get his massive frame off the ground. After a few minutes of slipping and grunting it worked and we were both standing.

"Where is Bob?" I asked as we slowly start walking towards home. He's limping and leaning heavily on me. "I saw Betty on the way here."

"I'm sorry honey, but Bob is gone." He said, deep sadness choking his voice.

"Gone? How?" I clung to his arm and focused on putting one step in front of the other.

"He was also bitten by this thing... when I tried to defend him, it gave me a bite. Then dragged him away, chains, harness and all. Betty shook free and took off," his French accent strong, as it always was when he became emotional.

"Bitten by what? A wolf?" I said looking down at his bloody leg. It seems to have clotted up, thank goodness an artery wasn't hit.

"No. Not a wolf. Did your grandmother in New Orleans tell you tales of a man with a wolf's head? The Rougarou? Mon dieu," he said.

"Yes, if I didn't go to church, she told me the Rougarou would come for me. Every kid in my neighbourhood was terrified into good behaviour with stories about the legendary monster. So. You are trying to tell me you were bit by what. A Cajun werewolf?" I asked in disbelief.

As if to accent my question, the howling started up again. I heard the rapid pounding of paws behind us, but as I turned ready to fight, I saw it was just Daisy. Thank goodness.

We were almost home and Benoit was picking up the pace,

"Louisa, I'm not imagining anything. It had a human body with long claws on its hands and a wolf's head."

I didn't respond immediately, but tried to remember the story my grandmother told me, always trying to frighten me into going to those long boring Catholic services. Some part of the story was niggling at my brain.

We were at the barn now and Betty was waiting at the door. I leaned Benoit against the side wall to let her into the barn and her stall. Luckily her heated bucket was already filled with water, so I just tossed some hay at her. She calmed down as soon as she started munching. But her eyes flicked in confusion at the empty stall beside her.

Grabbing a hold of Benoit again, we staggered into our house and I set him down on the couch. He pulled off his chainsaw pants and snow gear while I got some warm water, iodine and bandages. It did look like a creature had taken a chunk out of his leg. After cleaning it up and disinfecting it, I dressed him in his flannel pjs and gave him a glass of scotch. I rarely drink but I got one for myself as well.

I remember my grandmother's story clearer now. The heat of the whiskey cleared my mind and boiled in my mouth.

"Do you remember the rest of the legend Benoit? The part about how the Rougarou is under the spell for 101 days? Then after drawing human blood the curse is transferred to his victim?" I took a big gulp of my scotch and looked at him.

His eyes grew wide. He remembered. A new shiver rippled through me.

19

—————

ABOUT "A ROMANIAN TRADITION"

~

First published: October 2019
Scary Snippets Halloween Edition

DELLA MARIE SULLIVAN is a guest author in this collection, and she is also my mother. We shared a TOC in the Scary Snippets Halloween anthology of shorts.

DELLA MARIE SULLIVAN IS A MOTHER-OF-FOUR, voracious reader, and memoir writer. She is slave to an enormous Maine Coon Cat and addicted to the thrall of thriller novels.

20

────────

A ROMANIAN TRADITION

BY DELLA MARIE SULLIVAN

The rusty creak of the lid brought her out of her long sleep. It took a moment to shake off the cobwebs and she chuckled to herself as the black spiders ran for cover, racing up to the small slit of light and over the lip of the bed. Thank goodness, the countess thought, for this new technology. The coffin top was rigged (thanks Alexa) to open three hours before the stroke of midnight on the last day of the month of October.

Hopefully, this would give her enough time, to find her makeup, getting rid of the deathly pale of her face that 12 months of the year in the absolute dark took on her complexion. Twelve sips of human nectar would bring back her rosy cheeks and blood-red lips. Or maybe this year it would take more glasses of her special red wine; age took its toll in many ways. A long relieving stretch of her limbs and the thought of refreshment made her feel almost like her old self. She had to hurry as it was her turn to host the Ghoul party, which thankfully, was her responsibility once every fifty years. Her small group of royalty, consisting of Counts and Countesses and Barons, flying in from all corners of the world, had to look after their own special nutrition. For her a successful party was a quick walk to the corner store, selecting potato chips, cheezies, eggy sandwiches, and a few veggie trays. Even those of vampiric persuasion enjoyed salty snacks.

The sound of the trapdoor opening made her jump.

"Jenny, look what I found. This looks like an old wooden coffin, and maybe there is a vampire inside." He rubbed his hands in anticipation.

"Jimmy, you know that vampires don't exist. Just because it is Hallowe'en doesn't mean you can scare me. Get away from there. We are supposed to be looking for the old cedar box that Aunt Mable said was up here in the attic, and full of great costumes we could wear. We have to hurry or we will miss the beginning of the Spooky Night teen party at the community centre."

"Quit yelling, I'm coming," Jimmy said as he took a long last look over his shoulder at the dusty old

Container. "We don't have any garlic or silver bullets, anyway."

"Vampires don't die with that stuff; it has to be a wooden stake through the heart. That is, if they existed at all, which they DON'T. There is lots of good stuff in this old box. The costumes smell good too, want to be Superman or a witch, or a sorcerer, or a space alien. Or, hey, here is a long black cape, you could go as a vampire.

"Yeah, and I'm going to call myself, 'Count Suck Your Blood'", Jimmy hooted, laughing so hard he fell down and something made of glass shattered.

On hearing their voices, the countess shrank a bit back inside her coffin. She wasn't prepared yet to get her supper. But knowing where a large group of children would assemble just made her dream night of all Hallowed nights.

21

ABOUT "A BUG IN AMBER ALERT"

~

First published: October 2019
        Scary Snippets Halloween Edition

DURING THE DARK OF HALLOWEEN, *when little humans masquerade as all sorts of creatures, what can walk among us undetected?*

22

A BUG IN AMBER ALERT

BY ANGELIQUE FAWNS

There is only one night a year I can effectively hunt for what's been taken from me. Halloween. When else can you go from door-to-door and peer in at the lives of your neighbours? It is also the only day of the year I don't get odd stares. Parents shielding the eyes of their children from my face. Babies crying if they do get a close look.

It's not that I'm ugly per se... If you can see beneath the warts and unruly hair that insists on growing out of them, I have quite a pleasant visage. Green eyes, thick dark hair, but I am plagued by those damn warts, and I can't pluck the hair any faster than it grows. My face was unmarred till puberty, so my daughter is still beautiful, her inherited proclivities won't be evident for a few more years.

I cast a spell of spider infestation on the neighbours who called child services. What ordinary human understands that dancing naked under the moon into the wee hours of the night is healthy for the young? I had no more luck explaining the late dancing to the government child welfare officials than I did the contents of our fridge. Frog nuggets, thistle weed salad, and newt soup are delicacies. They took my daughter away and placed her in a foster home, denying me visitation or even allowing me to know her whereabouts.

Perhaps I shouldn't have flung vases, coats, and plates at them with my poltergeist incantation.

My local coven tried to locate her through lost and found rituals - but no luck. It's been almost a month since they took her, so I've resorted to old-school pounding of the pavement. Peeking in windows and flying above backyards has proven fruitless, but I have high hopes for tonight. With a bit of good fortune, child protective services haven't placed her too far out of my community.

Heading out the door, I join the throngs of little monsters, super-heroes, witches and cartoon characters. The fall leaves smell like hope, and the wind carries the cool of possibility.

"Lady, great costume," a dad with three Ninja Turtles in tow, hollers.

I smile and tip my pointed hat. At each house, I walk up the side-walk behind excited chattering groups of children and peer in as the doors open. Jack-o-lanterns leer at me in co-hoots on porch tables. So far, I haven't seen her ethereal face dishing out candy behind a door, or gotten a glimpse of the jacket she was wearing when she was taken.

Perhaps she will be out trick-or-treating herself? Skipping down the sidewalk with new school friends dressed in a billowy pink princess dress, or have the bones of a human skull painted on her face? I can't imagine she is happy being forced to eat the uninspired menu of the non-magical, and attending regular school. Spelling instead of spells, Math instead of magic.

When she comes into full power, her host family will be in trou-ble. But I have hours yet... the night is young.

23

ABOUT "MODEL CITIZEN"

First published: March 2021
From the Yonder 2 by War Monkey Publications

JENNY PERRY CARR is a guest author in this collection, and she crafts a chilling tale based on a true story.

JENNY PERRY CARR is a molecular neurobiologist by day, budding sci-fi/horror writer at night, which sounds much like the beginnings of a superhero's bio. But alas, her only superpower is remembering random facts, like the human body contains trillions of microorganisms that outnumber our own cells by 10 to 1!

24

MODEL CITIZEN: A DEADLY TALE OF BEAUTY

BY JENNY PERRY CARR

*L*iz Bath was a monster. A mammoth adversary to contend with. Known the world over as a woman to fear, her body was a weapon, and her looks could kill. She was a model after all.

Warm oil ran down her spine as a masseuse dribbled the elixir from a wooden bowl. Her statuesque figure draped over the massage table. She had a slender frame that stood more than six-feet tall. Women envied her lengthy legs, and men desired them. A behemoth in the modeling world. Nothing could stop her.

The orange glow from the candlelight accentuated her dewy skin. Tendrils of incense hung in the air, and recorded sounds of the forest filled her ears. She drew in a deep breath and let herself sink deeper into relaxation.

The masseuse kneaded her back, first in slow tender strokes, then harder, using her elbow to grind into her muscles. Liz gritted her teeth as the masseuse attempted to release weeks of tension. As the pain reached a peak, she clenched her fist, nails digging into her palm. Her eyes fluttered as she languished in the moment. She smirked in arousal.

A knock broke the serenity of the spa-like atmosphere.

"Not now," she roared, without raising her head from the table.

The masseuse stopped and pulled away. Liz narrowed her eyes and shot her a chilling glance.

"Did I tell you we were finished?"

"Sorry, ma'am." The masseuse resumed her massage, moving to her upper leg. Liz exhaled and relaxed again.

"Ma'am? It's important," her assistant's muffled voice said through the door, her knocking persistent. She had instructed Jane, her assistant, not to disturb her during her massages. This time was sacred.

"Someone better be dead." She sighed and lifted up, resting on her elbows. The masseuse backed away.

The mousey woman with chestnut hair and drab off-the-rack clothing appeared. She practically blended into the coffee-colored woodwork. Jane fidgeted with her well-worn day planner, several inches thick, with notes that stuck out at all angles.

Liz got up and patted down her flawless naked skin, wiping off the ruddy oil. She slipped on a silk robe behind an ornate abalone Qing Dynasty changing screen. She cinched her jet-black mane into a high, tight ponytail, which accentuated her prominent cheekbones and snowy complexion.

"*And*? What is so important?" She scowled at the assistant.

"Ms. Bath, a detective... A detective here to see you."

A detective? Liz raised a pointed eyebrow.

"Oh? Regarding?" She emerged from behind the screen, hands firmly planted on her hips, and stared down her timid secretary.

"A-a-a missing girl," Jane said, pushing her black-framed glasses up the bridge of her nose.

"Why do they want to talk to me? How does this involve the agency?" She tilted her head.

Jane shrugged. *Useless.*

"He's waiting in the conference room on 6." Jane pointed towards the elevator.

"Let him wait. I need a shower. I'm not presentable. I'll be down when I'm down." She flitted a dismissive hand at the assistant.

~

Liz flung the drapes open in her penthouse living room, looking out onto the New York skyline. Harsh daylight flooded the space, and she squinted. She owned the entire building and lived in the two-floor penthouse apartment above her company, a nice perk of being the boss. Disruptions irritated her as her packed schedule allowed only limited time for herself. This put a crimp in her day.

She lingered in the apartment, taking her time showering and primping. *Make the detective wait.* Liz grew accustomed to her power and enjoyed making people squirm. Waiting for long periods aggravated them most. She liked exposing their raw nerves and seeing how they would react under pressure. It gave her vital information about their character.

Many called her a cold bitch. But if one were describing the traits of a man, they would use terms like strong, decisive, and successful. She resented the double standard, but, none-the-less, she ruled her industry, making a fortune for herself.

None of her money came from her affluent father. He died in her European homeland when she was young, and her mother followed soon thereafter. Liz floated from relative to relative until she was of age, but ruthless relations squandered her parental wealth, leaving her penniless by eighteen. Liz broke ties with everyone. She found she had a knack for business, and success came easily to her. She ventured to the United States, and little remained of her accent. An opulent upbringing groomed her for a life of rubbing elbows with New York's elite and powerful. She blended right in. Manhattan had no idea what walked amongst them.

The elevator door slid open, and Liz stepped out onto the 6th floor of the industrial chic office building. She was an imposing woman, both in stature and in spirit. Irregular triangles of black and white fabric covered her body. The contemporary, geometric dress looked more like it belonged on a Paris runway than in an office, but she wore it well with confidence. She strode down the hall towards the conference room, styled in concrete and wood. Office staff stiffened at the sight of her. Silence fell over the open floor plan as she passed.

The detective leaned in and examined the artwork on the wall. He reached out a hand to inspect the canvas as she entered.

"Don't touch that," she said.

He flinched. "You startled me. Sorry, I just..." He smiled awkwardly with a boyish charm and pointed at the painting. "Is this real?"

"It *is* a painting." She crossed her arms and shifted her weight to one hip.

"I mean, is this the original?"

Stupid cop. Clearly, he hadn't picked up on her condescension.

"Yes. A gift from a dear friend." She gazed at the piece. She adored the bold strokes and vivid colors of this particular Van Gogh. *The gnarled trees look just like our vineyard.*

"Wow. Impressive."

"Indeed." She offered her hand. "I'm Liz Bath, president and CEO of Liz Bath modeling agency. But I'm sure you were already well aware of that given your profession."

His eyes widened as she shook his hand with a firm grip.

"Indeed." He parroted her words. Perhaps he had detected her insult. "Detective Florez."

"What brings you to our agency, Detective?" She gestured for him to sit down at the large mahogany table.

"I'm following up on a case that's gone cold." He removed a photo from a manila folder and slid it across the table. The pretty young girl in the headshot stared at her. She must have been fifteen, sixteen, with a sparkle in her eyes.

"Molly Perkins has been missing for over five years," he said.

"And this involves me, how?" She pushed the image back to the detective and crossed her hands on her lap.

"There were reports that Molly came to the city to become a model." He flipped the headshot over. On the back, written in purple ink, was the word *Bath* and a phone number. His finger tapped on the digits. "This reaches the reception desk of your agency. We called and haven't been able to gather much information from your staff."

"They don't give out information to just anyone."

"The NYPD isn't just anyone, ma'am." He flipped the photo back over and shoved it across the table. "I need to know if Molly worked with you. It might help us generate a lead. Does she look familiar?"

She scoffed and smirked. "Are you joking? Do you realize how many girls come through this agency?" She flicked the photo back towards him.

"No, I don't. Enlighten me."

Liz rose and started out the door. "Are you coming?" She paused.

He grabbed the photo and followed quickly behind. She glided down the hallway past several posh offices, leading him through a maze of stylish cubicles and modern meeting rooms.

"Thousands of prospective models inundate Liz Bath every year, vying for a contract. Of those that submit headshots, we only bring in a few hundred for further review. And of those, we only hire a handful for our clients' specific needs." She waved her hand at the busy workspace.

"Girls travel here from all around the world. Some want to escape and start over and don't give us their real names. Some are runaways hiding from their past. Many of these girls want to disappear for one reason or another. Who am I to stop them?"

She strolled to an office and rapped her knuckles on the door-frame to announce her presence, though everyone already realized she was there.

"This is Shea. She can help you search through our records for this Milly girl." She gestured towards the exceedingly slender woman in couture attire seated in front of a computer. Shea nodded in agreement.

"Molly," the detective said.

"What?"

"Her name is Molly. Molly Perkins."

Did he really just correct me? Who cares what her name was? Is.

"Sure. Whatever." She rolled her eyes and walked away before he could say another word.

~

At the elevators, Liz pushed the call button and waited to go back up to her office. The doors opened, and she got in and pushed 9.

"Ms. Bath?" An arm stuck in, forcing the steel doors to retract.

She sighed. Detective Florez stepped in.

"Done already? The receptionist can show you out." She pressed the button for 9 repeatedly. The doors closed.

"Not done yet. Still have a few more questions."

"I'm not sure what to tell you. I have no answers."

She crossed her arms and rolled her weight to one hip. The floor indicator overhead pinged as they passed the 7th floor. *How do I get rid of him?*

"Actually, I have some other photos I'd like to show you." He pulled a headshot from his folder. A young woman smiled at her innocently. "This is Julie Davidson. And this..." He pulled out another photo of a girl. The indicator binged as they passed 8. "This is Angela Washington."

"Let me guess. Missing?" she said sarcastically.

"Ma'am? Do you think this is a joke?"

The elevator sounded one last time, and the doors opened. *Finally.* Liz headed to her corner office, knowing he would follow her like a puppy. She waited to reply until they were in the closed office.

"I take my business deadly serious. That is no joke. I see what you are getting at. What you're insinuating. That somehow *my* agency is involved." She sat down behind the enormous desk. The detective opted to stand. "I don't take these unfounded accusations lightly." She pounded her index finger into the desktop. "Trying to link these girls' disappearances to my business could tarnish my reputation."

She withdrew a cigarette from a carved wooden box on her desk and lit it with a silver butane lighter. She drew in a long drag and tossed the lighter down on the desk. This line of questioning made her tense. The nicotine calmed her nerves. A cloud of smoke wafted towards the detective as she exhaled.

"Frankly, ma'am, I'm more concerned about finding these girls than your business," he said matter-of-factly. "I'd like to talk with more of your staff to see if they know anything about them."

"Very well." She waved the cigarette at him. "Talk to whoever you must."

"Thank you." He nodded, stuffing the photos back into the folder, and padded out of her office.

This was problematic. She really didn't need a detective sniffing around her agency. She leaned back in the chair and weighed her options, taking another long drag. She sat up and pushed a button on her phone.

"Get in here," she barked at the intercom.

"Yes, ma'am," the tinny voice replied through the speaker.

Within moments, Jane appeared in the doorway, straightening her skirt, which always seemed crooked.

"Close the door behind you."

Jane obliged and sat on one of the chairs facing the massive desk.

"Pull all the information we have on Molly Perkins, Julie Davidson, and Angela Washington. Photos, applications, interview briefs, client jobs. Destroy everything. I don't want a single record of them to exist. Erase them."

"Ma'am?"

"Do it. And keep that detective out of Studio C. His presence vexes me. Do whatever you can to make him leave."

Jane finished writing the instructions and shut the day planner. She nodded acknowledgement of her orders and scurried out of the office.

The phone rang.

"Yes?"

It was Carl.

"Today? *Now*?"

Carl ran her casting department. He oversaw the review of all applicants. He had been with her for years, her eyes and ears in the company. When he found a girl matching the appropriate criteria, he would call Liz to personally interview them. Today, he found a winner.

"Your timing isn't great, Carl. Okay, I'm coming."

Liz took one last drag from her cigarette before throwing it onto the concrete hallway floor. She crushed the butt with her stiletto and got into the elevator. She pushed the button for the ground floor. As the elevator descended, she tried to let the stress of the detective slip away and became eager at the thought of a new young beauty. She took a deep breath. The anticipation made her giddy.

Bing. The elevator door opened, and her icy visage melted into a phony warm smile. The girl sat alone in the waiting room. *Indeed, she fit the bill.* Young, about 16, but her looks could pass for 21. Liz drew in the smell of her hair as she scooped the young woman by the elbow. She pulled her from the chair and lead her down the hallway close by her side. The girl stood nearly head-to-head with Liz. Pretty, but far from runway material, or even print modeling for that matter. Perfect.

"You must be Stacy. I'm so happy to meet you. I'm Liz." She gave the girl a one-armed half-hug as she guided her to an office.

"Hi. I, uh, thanks. Yes, I'm Stacy." The girl fidgeted in her grasp, probably wondering why the CEO held her by the arm and took a personal interest in her.

"I'd like to find out everything about you." She led Stacy to an empty office. The girl was like a doe on the opening day of hunting season. "Sit. Let's talk."

"Is this what you usually do?"

"Usually? No. But for special girls, I like to do the interview myself." Flattery typically calmed nerves.

A toothy grin filled the girl's face.

"It's just that I've never done this before. Modeling, I mean." *Obvi-*

ously. She wouldn't have made it past reception in most agencies, but Liz Bath wasn't most agencies.

"Completely fine. It's a thrill to pluck a diamond from the rough. I'm glad you came here first." Liz sat across the desk from her and took hold of the girl's hands. Her supple skin felt like velvet beneath her fingertips. She took a slow, measured breath.

"What made you choose the Liz Bath agency?" She could always use a little flattery herself.

"It's the best. Like, the best of the best, of the best, of the best."

"And you thought you were the best?" Liz cocked her head to the side.

The girl's cheeks burned crimson. "Well, I, uh, I mean, I wanted the best representation. It's not that I'm the best..." Her voice trailed off.

Liz clasped her hands hard and locked eyes with the girl.

"You are the best. If you're going to be a Bath model, the answer to that question should always be, 'Yes, I am the best'." Stacy nodded and looked down.

Liz pulled her forward on the desk.

"You can't doubt yourself. If you want to succeed in this business, hold your head high with confidence. You must believe you are the most beautiful girl in every room you enter."

Stacy smiled. Her clear blue eyes lit up her entire face.

Liz released her hands and sat back in the oversized executive chair.

"Now, tell me your story."

"My story?"

"Where are you from? What do you like to do? Family? Friends? Aspirations? Spare no details."

"There isn't much, I guess. I'm from Connecticut. Not much family left, though. I'm an only child, no brothers or sisters, and my parents passed away when I was little." Her eyes lost their sparkle and filled with sadness. "I've been living with my aunt in Bridgeport, but she got a new boyfriend who I don't like. The way he looks at me, especially when I get out of the shower." She shuddered. Liz listened intently. "I left. I don't think they'll care one bit. They might not even notice I'm gone." She fidgeted in her seat, probably questioning if she had shared too much.

"Excellent." Liz needed to qualify that statement. "It was excellent you got away from that. And why modeling?"

"My mama always told me I was pretty. So, I thought..."

"That you could make some money with your face."

Stacy laughed nervously. "Something like that."

"Alright then."

"Is that it? Did I do okay?"

Liz patted the girl's hand. "You did great. Let's get you to Hair and Makeup and have some test photos taken."

Carl waited at the office door. He smoothed his well-groomed salt and pepper beard.

"Give Stacy here the royal treatment. Then take her down to Studio C." Liz squeezed Stacy's shoulders, and the girl gave Carl a big confident smile.

Liz raised her eyebrows at Carl. "Good eye, Carl. Good eye."

He winked at Liz and led the girl away. She had a bounce in her step as she followed him down the corridor. At least the girl was happy. For now.

TODAY TURNED out to be much better than Liz first thought. She grinned as she awaited the elevator, pleased with herself and her little charade. The doors slid open.

"Ms. Bath. Just person I wanted to talk to." Detective Florez stood inside.

Good God. She scowled. How quickly her mood soured. She reluctantly got in. The button for 9 already glowed. *Great.*

"You're *still* here? Didn't get what you needed?"

"Not yet. I'm heading up to meet with Jane now."

Liz pressed the door-close button forcefully several times. *Why hadn't Jane gotten rid of him yet? She had better get this job done, and fast.*

"Since I have you trapped in the elevator..."

She glanced at him sideways. "Excuse me?"

He laughed. "I mean, I have a few minutes of your *precious* time to ask you some more questions." This time he dealt out the sarcasm. She didn't enjoy being on the receiving end.

"Okay."

"Great." He pulled out a small tattered notebook from his inside jacket pocket and clicked his pen. "Where were you the night of April tenth?"

"How should I know?" She crossed her arms. His question angered her. "You'd have to ask Jane. She carries my entire life around in that planner of hers. I don't have time to keep track of details like that. I have people for that."

"Your people aren't very forthcoming with information."

"Then they're good people, no?" She played coy.

The doors slid open at the 9th floor, and she sauntered out, away from Detective Florez. She didn't notice Jane waiting and crashed into her assistant, sending her planner flying, the contents scattered on the floor. Liz stormed past with a huff, leaving Jane to deal with the mess, both the strewn papers and the detective.

She glanced over her shoulder and saw the defective kneel beside Jane, helping the assistant pick up all the fallen pages. *How chivalrous.* She rolled her eyes.

She slumped into her office chair and pulled out a large folding mirror from her desk. As she opened it, little bright lights popped on around the perimeter of the glass. Liz looked at her features, running a finger delicately under her eye. *Desperately in need of renewal.* The excitement of the investigator put a wrinkle in her plans, and apparently on her face. A newly formed crow's foot emanated from the corner of her eye. She snapped the mirror shut and threw it back into the drawer. She didn't need a reminder of her age. Soon it wouldn't matter.

She considered the risk of going through with things with Florez still in the building. But her need erased any doubt within moments. A treatment was well overdue.

The phone on her desk sprang to life.

"Yes?" she answered. Her hard face softened. "Perfect timing. Studio C. I'll be down in a moment."

She walked to the door. Jane rushed in and almost ran into her. Again.

"Ma'am," her voice hurried and nervous, "we have a problem. A serious problem."

Liz grabbed Jane's arm.

Before she could ask what, Detective Florez burst in.

"Do you mind explaining this to me?" He held a handwritten note.

She let go of Jane, white marks already visible on the assistant's forearm. "I have no idea what that is." She answered honestly.

"Ma'am, it's—" Jane said.

"Shhh. Let the man speak."

"Apparently this is a note written by your assistant." He read aloud. "*Full delete M Perkins, J Davidson, A Washington.* Are you still going to tell me you don't know these girls?"

Jane wiped tears from her eyes and started whimpering. Florez glared with accusation.

Liz smoothed her hair and calmed her breathing. She wouldn't let him excite her.

"I merely asked my assistant to check for any records on them."

"Delete? That doesn't sound like a check. If you don't start answering me straight, I'm going to call for backup, and we'll tear this office apart. Damn your reputation."

She stepped forward to face Florez, well within his personal space, and poked her index finger against his chest.

"You will do no such thing. You will not threaten me. Unless you have more than a worthless scrap of paper, get the hell out of my building. And don't come back without a warrant."

She returned to her desk, picked up the receiver, and punched in a few buttons on the keypad. "Security?"

Florez held up his hands in surrender. "Okay, okay. No need for that. I'll go. But I will be back with that warrant."

He stormed out. Jane continued to sob to herself.

"Pull yourself together if you want to keep your job."

Jane nodded and sniffled, looking at her with red eyes.

"Now I have a job to do."

THINGS SHOULDN'T HAVE GOTTEN that heated with the detective. She made a point to fly under the radar of law enforcement. But now, she had drawn its attention. She would have to deal with that later.

Liz pushed through the stairwell door, far too impatient to wait for the elevator. The walk down would calm her mind and collect her thoughts.

She flew down the stairs, her heels clacking on each concrete step. The sound echoed down the into the depths of the building. Numbers on each landing got smaller and smaller until she came to a door labeled B. The basement. She swiped her keycard through the security strip. A red light switched to green, and the door buzzed open.

The agency's photo studios were underground, in the lower level. They found the space convenient for staged photography with no natural light pollution. Twenty-foot ceilings allowed for the creation of elaborate sets, complete with rigging for custom lighting design.

Liz also liked the privacy of the basement. While a few people worked in the studio from time to time, they didn't have shoots that often, so usually the lower level remained quiet.

But today, Studio C sprung to life. Liz entered and found Carl seated on a couch at the back. He leaned with one arm up on the sofa. He wore an impeccable ensemble from that new designer's line they previewed last fall. Carl's taste in fashion paralleled hers. Another thing she loved about him.

"She's ready for you." He extended an arm out towards the set, like an offering.

Liz stood by Carl and patted his shoulder.

"Nice work, Carl. This is a good one. I can feel it."

Long, billowing, white chiffon hung from the ceiling, tied up with white cording to create extravagant textures and folds. Complex lighting bounced and reflected off the fabric, filling the studio with a luminous glow. Liz watched the photographer work, guiding the young novice.

Stacy wore a sleeveless ivory dress. The gauzy, deep V-neck ended just above her navel. They fashioned a makeshift belt from a piece of the same cording that styled the set, giving the outfit a polished, coordinated look. She twirled around. The cloth swirled around Stacy's ankles and bare feet. The thin fabric left little to the imagination. Strands of hair fell from the loose up do and outlined her cherubic face. The makeup artist brought out the blue in her eyes with deep, smokey, eye makeup. While not gorgeous, she was lovely, innocent, and her naïve smile infectious. Liz smirked as she watched her pose for the camera.

The photographer caught sight of Liz and paused.

"Don't let me interrupt. She seems like a natural." Liz pointed towards the girl and smiled.

Stacy looked genuinely happy, having the time of her life. She spun around again and again, until she stumbled with dizziness, and giggled.

"I think we're done here. I got the shots." The photographer pulled the camera from the tripod and packed up his gear. The bright fill lights switched off and the studio dimmed.

Stacy's smile faded, and she tugged at her hair, unsure what to do as everyone shuffled around her.

"Excellent. Add these shots to my private collection." Liz shifted her attention to the girl.

"Clear the studio," Liz shouted.

Carl rounded up the last of the staff and the photographer and gave thumbs up to Liz as he swung the large metal door of the studio shut with a clang.

"Should I go with Carl?"

"No. I thought we could talk a little more."

Liz circled around the girl.

"Okay." Stacy shifted nervously and crossed one foot over the other.

"How did you like your makeover?" Liz's voice was slow and measured.

Stacy lit up. "Oh, it was so much fun. I already learned a lot." She beamed. "Like what colors go with my eyes, and how to put on eyeliner." She waved her arms excitedly as she talked.

"Let's take a good look at you." Liz trailed a finger down the girl's shoulder. Her movements were deliberate like a predator sizing up their prey. She clasped Stacy's hands and gracefully stretched her arms out wide, assessing the dress. "Beautiful." She eyed the girl.

Liz moved behind her.

"How is the fit?" She tugged firmly at the shoulders of the dress and cinched the fabric at the back.

"Fine, I think. It feels good."

Liz slipped her hand around the girl's waist and untied the white cord.

"Let's see how you look without the belt."

"Okay."

Liz wrapped the ends of the cord tightly around each of her hands. In a swift move, she flipped the cord over the girl's head and yanked tight against the girl's neck.

Stacy lost her footing and fell against Liz's chest.

She pulled the cording tighter.

Stacy struggled to free herself. Her fingers clawed at the cord squeezing her neck, unable to loosen the rope. She choked, gasping for air, unable to speak or scream. She turned red, and her eyes widened.

Liz remained calm. She pulled the rope firmly. She leaned back, squeezing the life from her.

Stacy kicked her feet violently. She reached her hands behind her head, trying to grab her attacker.

Liz pulled her backwards deeper into the set, never easing up on her grip.

The girl's lips went blue, and her eyes bulged, the whites staining red with broken blood vessels.

Stacy flailed her arms out. She caught a section of the white hanging chiffon, pulling it taut. A ripping sound echoed through the studio as the girl pulled the fabric.

Liz held firm, knowing the struggle would end soon. Experience and patience.

The naïve girl struggled helplessly.

Stacy's hold on the fabric loosened. The girl's hand went limp, her body followed.

Liz lowered her to the ground and dropped the cording.

The ripped chiffon, still in Stacy's hand, gave way and wafted down from the rafters, piling around the girl's dead body.

Liz straightened her dress and pulled the large studio door open.

Carl waited outside, leaning against the wall, chewing on a toothpick.

"That was quick. You didn't waste any time." He smirked.

"I'm running out of time. Make this fast. Get her processed *now*."

"During the day? Are you crazy? We have an office full of people above us." He pointed up and wrinkled his face.

"Figure it out. I can't solve all your problems. Make it happen."

He raised his hands. "Alright. I get it. Hurry. Rush. Now. Fast," he said sarcastically. He flicked his toothpick on the floor. "I'm on it." Carl disappeared inside Studio C, and the metal door swung shut.

She smoothed a few stray hairs that had freed themselves during the fray. She straightened her dress and headed back upstairs.

In the elevator, she swiped her keycard and pressed P. The penthouse. The day had exhausted her, and she needed to retreat to her sanctuary to recharge. She hoped Carl would work fast, as she couldn't wait much longer. Her patience wore thin.

The door opened directly into the foyer of her penthouse. The grand double staircase wrapped around either side of the entryway. Lavish antiques from around the globe and across the centuries adorned the art deco apartment.

Liz stepped out of the elevator. The upper floor of the penthouse held the master suite and guest rooms. To the left, the apartment opened into a large dining room, and to the right, a spacious living room. In front of her, underneath the stairs, a corridor led to her library. She walked straight ahead.

Darkness shrouded the books. The heavy green velvet drapes blocked the afternoon sun. She lit the wick on a gilded lamp. The yellow flame filled the room with flickering shadows. Leather-bound tomes lined the shelves from floor to ceiling.

Liz removed an ornate glass bottle top from the decanter on a side table and poured herself a drink. She lifted the tumbler, giving an imaginary toast to herself.

"Egészségedre," she said. "To my health."

She swallowed the caustic liquid down in one gulp. She winced. After all these years, she still didn't like the harsh taste of liquor, but she needed it to relax.

She lounged in the leather armchair and waited for Carl, laying back, letting the liquid in her belly ease her tension. She found it difficult to rest, knowing what was coming.

ALMOST AN HOUR PASSED when Carl knocked on the wooden doorframe to announce his presence.

"Finally." She sat up, waiting for his report.

"It's ready. And *finally*? Really? Maybe if it was night, but broad daylight? This took some magic to go undetected." Carl was her long-time employee and companion. He was the only one that could talk to her this way. He kept her honest.

"I'm just eager. It's been too long since the last." They walked down the hallway together.

"I understand. It's getting harder these days. It's not just about a paper trail. Now there's an internet footprint to deal with." He pulled her hand into the crook of his elbow as they headed up the staircase.

They entered the master suite. A large round tub in the middle of the floor dominated the bathroom. The crisp white porcelain was a stark contrast to the dark ebony tiled floors and walls.

Carl had already set everything up just as she liked it. Pillar candles on every surface cast long shadows across the room.

Liz untied her tight ponytail and let her black hair spill around her shoulders. She kicked off her shoes. Carl unzipped the back of her dress, and she let the designer piece fall to the floor. She wore no undergarments. She wasn't shy about her body.

Liz stepped over the rim of the large tub. Her legs slipped into the warm liquid. She sunk down into the bath until submerged to the neck.

Carl gave a quick bow and dismissed himself from the room as Liz settled into the comfort of the bath.

Thick red blood warmed her. Liz massaged the fluid into her skin. She relaxed her head back against the porcelain and sensed the life force from the young girl's blood enter her body. The years counted backwards on her face, restoring her beauty. Fine lines around her eyes and mouth softened and faded within moments. The luster in her cheeks heightened. Her glowing skin was radiant again.

Liz sunk deeper into the bath. The blood covered first her chin, then her mouth, her nose, eyes, until she was fully immersed. She held her breath for what seemed like minutes.

A muffled voice reverberated through the liquid. *Who dared to bother me during my ritual?* She lifted her head and wiped her eyes clear with a hand.

"Jesus Christ. What the hell is going on here?"

Detective Florez stood before her with Jane.

"I couldn't stop him. He has a warrant." She made excuses.

Florez's mouth hung agape, his eyes wide.

"Ma'am. Get out of the tub." Florez drew his gun from its holster and flicked the safety. "You're under arrest."

Liz slowly rose from the bloody bath. Red painted every inch of her.

"On what charge?" She stepped out, her perfect body naked standing before Florez.

"Ms. Bath, put some clothes on." He averted his eyes from her body, looking at the floor.

"Not until you tell me the charge."

"You're taking a fucking bath in blood. Where did this come from? Whose blood is this?"

"It's pigs' blood if you must know. It's a beauty regimen I follow."

"Bullshit. There is something going on here. Maybe I'll finally get some answers from you downtown."

Liz stepped towards the detective.

"Don't move, ma'am." He pointed the gun at her, shifting his gaze up to take aim, but looked down again, uncomfortable with her nakedness.

"Well, which is it? Get clothes? Or don't move? I can't do both," she said.

Florez turned to Jane. His gun's aim drifted to the floor. "Give her a towel."

Liz stepped forward and grabbed the barrel of the detective's gun while he was distracted. Her advance caught him off guard, and he struggled to gain control of the weapon. Her strength rivaled his.

Blood dripped off her and pooled around her feet. In the struggle, Florez slipped and fell to the floor, taking her with him. Blood smeared across the tile. She gripped the gun, and he yanked it back, trying to gain the upper hand.

They wrestled for control of the gun. Neither could get any leverage as they slid in the blood. Florez wrenched the barrel towards Liz, and she fought to twist his arm away.

Bang. A shot echoed in the large bathroom.

Jane clutched her stomach. Her face wrinkled. Blood oozed out from between her fingers. She dropped down onto her feet and slumped over onto the ground.

Liz grabbed the gun from Florez and pointed the barrel underneath his chin. He held up his hands.

"Did you really think you were going to stop me?"

Liz got up, gun still pointed at the detective.

"I've crossed paths with many more cunning than you. I'm 460 years old, and it's going to take more than you to stop me."

Florez narrowed his eyes. "What are you going to do? I got a warrant. The station knows I'm here."

She lunged forward at him, and he flinched.

"You're just a scared little boy." She waved the gun in his face and flipped open his coat with the barrel. She reached into his breast pocket and ripped out the folded papers.

"A warrant. How quaint." She opened the papers with one hand, leaving a trail of bloody prints on the pages.

"Ahhh. Judge Hopkins? We go way back. 1971? 72? My youth may surprise him, but I'll make this go away. I always do."

Liz threw down the papers and advanced on Florez. She whisked him up off the ground by the neck, and he scrambled to regain his footing.

"Now the question is, what to do with you?" She cocked her head to the side. She tossed the gun across the floor and cackled with laughter.

Her demeanor changed so dramatically from the poised woman in the office to this monstrous creature. With a still flawless and beautiful body, her true horrific nature showed through bloody, matted hair and a gnarled expression. A monster lurked within.

Florez struggled beneath her grip, but the bath had strengthened and enlivened her. She dragged him to the tub and forced his body down to the edge of the porcelain.

"This is what I'll do with you." She pushed his head down to the surface of the blood. He struggled, but she didn't falter.

She leaned down, her cheek almost touching his, and whispered in his ear through gritted teeth.

"I will add your blood to my bath as I have done with thousands. Your life, your essence, will feed my soul and restore me. And who will remember you? No one."

Liz grabbed Florez by the back of the hair and yanked his head back. She raised her other hand, and in one adept stroke, sliced her long nails along across his neck. Thin red lines appeared on his flesh. Blood seeped from the wounds and flowed out in a steady stream.

She released him from her hold. He frantically pawed at his neck in a futile attempt to close the wounds. His eyes widened. But soon he relaxed and slipped forward over the lip of the bath, his blood spilling into the tub.

Liz stood and looked over at her dead assistant. *Utterly useless.* She crouched beside her and brushed the dead woman's hands away, exposing the wound. Liz stuck her fingers into the hole in Jane's sweater and deep into the gunshot wound. She withdrew her hand, covered in fresh blood, and wiped it across her own cheeks.

Liz returned to the bath and ran a hand through the liquid. Florez' blood added renewed warmth to the bath. At least it wasn't cold yet. She climbed back in and slid down. Florez' lifeless body hung over her, his blood trickled into the tub in a melodic song of drips.

Liz smiled. It had been years since she had the blood of multiple victims in one day. She hadn't felt this good in years.

Just as she settled in, a rousing cough sounded at the door. Carl leaned against the doorframe.

"Someone's been busy, I see." Carl gestured to the dead bodies.

She sighed. "Couldn't be helped." She laid back down and closed her eyes.

"Mhmmm." He sounded doubtful.

"I need you to take care of these two." She waved a dismissive, bloody hand.

"Of course."

Carl turned to leave.

"And Carl?" She sat up and leaned on her crossed arms on the edge of the tub. Red streaks poured down the side of the white porcelain.

Carl looked back. "Yes?"

"Erase them." She grinned.

～

BY JENNY PERRY CARR

Epilogue

Based on a true story, *Model Citizen* is a modern retelling of the life of Elizabeth Bathory, a wealthy Hungarian woman, born in 1560. We know her from history as the most prolific female serial killer, with more than five hundred victims. Legend tells us that Elizabeth bathed in the blood of virgin girls to maintain her youth. This story imagines that Elizabeth not only preserved her youth but also lived well beyond her years, surviving to modern times. In reality, Elizabeth was tried for her crimes and imprisoned in 1611. She died in prison in 1614 at the age of 54.

25

ABOUT "THE METAMORPHOSIS"

~

First published: January 2021
Night Terrors Vol. 9

A TWIST on the vampire trope, what if the bloodsuckers originated from leeches?

26

THE METAMORPHOSIS

BY ANGELIQUE FAWNS

*S*eth hesitated before tossing the knife into the suitcase laying open on his antique mahogany four-poster bed. The ornate hunting blade; lamprey eels carved into the wood handle, fell squarely in the middle of the overflowing clothes. The artist's rendition of the jawless fish looked like Stephen King's version of a leech. Many toothed monsters. Oil lamps cast a dim light on the sweaters, shorts, t-shirts, and boxers in the well-worn leather luggage. The black bag was enormous, covered in travel stickers from farm shows all over North America, and holding up well for a 50-year-old item. He needed the space for his size 46 pants and XXXL shirts. *What was he supposed to pack for an experimental medical treatment?*

"Better to overpack than wish you'd brought your favorite sweats, eh Charlie?" Seth asked the miniature pig laying on the dog bed in the corner of his bedroom.

He'd inherited the knife, the suitcase, and an aggressive form of diabetes from his recently deceased father. Charlie squealed when he zipped the bag shut.

"You can't come little pig, but no worries, I got you a hog sitter."

He picked up a small morsel of chocolate on his bedside table and tossed it at her.

"I was saving this for a late-night snack, but if I'm serious about kicking this diabetes, I got to kick the sweet treats first."

Charlie's pink tongue snagged the chocolate. Seth painfully shrugged off his overalls and forced his swollen fingers to undo the snaps on his plaid shirt. He looked at the cornucopia of drugs on his bedside table. Aleve, Advil, Tylenol, CBD oil, even a tab or two of Oxy. He dry-swallowed an Advil, and climbed into bed.

"Time for some shuteye, pretty pig."

His potbellied pet laid her head down and gave a contented grunt.

"If this treatment works, Charlie, you and I can start jogging together. We could both use more exercise." The pig was already fast asleep, her jowls vibrating as she snored.

Seth was too nervous to fall asleep. He ran his hands over his belly. Gut fat on a thirty-year-old man was not healthy, even though he hid it pretty well on his 6ft 4inch frame. A year ago, he had moved back to the farm when his dad died unexpectedly. His Mom had already been gone for years. *Someone had to run the piggery farm.* But when it came time to send the fattened pork "to market"? Seth couldn't bring himself to slaughter any of them. The intelligence in their eyes; the way they played with each other; he half wished he could join them and roll around ecstatically in the mud.

But what kind of pig farmer can't kill a pig? He missed both his parents; he was annoyed he had to leave his job selling the farm's produce at the city market; and now he felt like a farming failure. So, he ate. And ate. And ate. He devoured everything except bacon.

Trying to force himself to sleep, he mentally envisioned his pigs jumping one-by-one over a haybale. There were 50 pigs on his farm, and he was busy naming them all.

"Jump Esmerelda! Okay Notorious P.I.G. you're up. Over you go, Bertha you need more speed to clear that hay." Seth mumbled until he was snoring like Charlie.

#

The next morning Dolores, his closest neighbor on their remote country road, pulled into his driveway in a beat-up Ranger 4x4. She ran a tanning and mud bath business, called Sun & Mud. Seth had yet to see many clients though, he had no idea how she kept it afloat. His front door banged shut.

"Get outta bed, you handsome hunk of manhood! You'se got yer appointment with the Diabetic Doc today," she hollered from the bottom of the stairs.

Scrambling out of bed, he pulled on his overalls and grabbed his suitcase. Charlie followed him down the stairs. Leaning provocatively in the doorway, Dolores was dressed in a thrift store prom dress. Pushing fifty, she wore a cheap pink wig, which matched the lace gown.

"How are you going to do farm chores dressed in that?" Seth asked.

"I'll take good care of your farm big man. Just come back to me good n' healthy so we can have a hot romance already." Dolores winked one over-mascaraed eye.

She sashayed over to pick up his suitcase sitting beside the front door. Charlie trotted into the kitchen to eat breakfast out of the automatic food-dispenser.

"Are you sure this Doctor knows what he's doing?" Seth asked, grabbing his wallet and keys off the antique buffet.

"I'm tellin' ya this healer guy works miracles! My brother had a bad case of the them diabetes and he got cured up right quick. It's a highly experimental top-secret treatment alright! You'll be thanking me with a deep kiss when y'all get back!"

Seth suppressed a shudder, following Dolores out to his truck. She threw the suitcase in like it was made of feathers. Though she wasn't the prettiest lady, she radiated strength and vitality. He was slightly terrified of her. But he couldn't keep taking care of his pigs if his feet were always sore. He needed to get his disease under control and this felt like a final "Hail Mary".

"Please take good care of Charlie and all my other pigs. The grain bins are full and the water troughs need to be refilled daily."

Seth fired up his old Ford 150. It was a beautiful fall day and the leaves were just beginning to turn. Wind ruffled his thick black hair.

The air was warm but his hands trembled on the wheel. He took deep breaths and forced himself not to turn the truck around. Somehow, he made it to the small public dock along the sands of the enormous and tumultuous lake. The grey waves crashed against the shore, looking inhospitable. A man stood on the dock with a Pontoon boat moored beside him.

Yanking the old leather suitcase behind him he walked slowly, hoping his legs wouldn't give way. The light spray from the lake waves was chilling. The lone figure on the dock didn't look much like a doctor. He was tall, bald and wearing ill-fitting surgical scrubs under a coyote fur jacket.

"Seth! Glad you could make it. I'm Doctor Damien. There is no ferry over to Serpent Island, so I'll transport you myself. True personalized service."

Dr. Damien gestured to the boat. It floated on the water thanks to big barrels attached to a wide deck, shaded by a tarp roof.

Seth stepped on the deck, wincing at the pain in his feet, as Dr. Damien quickly untied the boat and pushed off. Sitting down on the white bench at the back of the boat, he tried to keep his eyes firmly on the horizon. He hadn't eaten breakfast and acid curdled in his stomach. It was a relief hopping off the boat onto firm land when they got to the little island.

A bronzed muscular man, a foot taller and twice as wide as the doctor, waited for them on a decrepit wood dock. He was also bald and tanned, but had tribal tattoos decorating his skull.

"I'm Dan, the assistant. I hope your visit will be all transformative and shit."

"Transformative? You're not going to give me Ayahuasca or anything?" Seth wasn't the sort to sit in a teepee drinking a poisonous drug while hunting for his spirt animal.

"No, there'll be no hallucinogenic drugs, don't worry Seth,"" Dr. Damien said.

"Whatever." Dan grabbed Seth's suitcase from him and walked off the dock onto a gravel path.

Seth couldn't see any roads or cars on Serpent Island. From the water, it hardly looked big enough to be called an island with only one or two cottages on the white sand beach. The gravel path led into a forest and soon became a dirt trail. Pines swayed in the wind as they stepped over logs and branches strewn haphazardly on the path.

His anxiety mounted with every step. This was obviously not a typical medical center. *Was he being kidnapped? He might have made a big mistake. Could he get to his knife?*

"Let's waste no time, Dan will store your suitcase and you follow me," Dr. Damien said.

Panicked, he watched the tattooed man wheel his suitcase, and his knife, out of sight.

"Aren't we going to some sort of clinic? I was thinking nurses with pale yellow scrubs, bright lights and sterile equipment?" Seth wrung his sweaty hands.

"Your treatment will be unorthodox, but very effective. Have faith my handsome friend," Dr. Damien said.

Reluctantly, he followed the back of the Doctor's coyote fur jacket down a path deeper into the woods. The last of the sun's rays illuminated a murky pond. They stopped at the edge and Seth took a deep breath. A deep earthy smell; moss, mildew and the decay of long dead plants filled his nostrils. The water was a muddy brown with cat tails and water grass festooning the edges.

"Time to strip down to your skivvies," Dr. Damien said.

"What kind of treatment is this?" Seth asked, shivering and pulled his shirt tighter around him.

"A breakthrough way of treating extreme diabetes that combines an age-old remedy along with a drug that I, myself, developed. Patent coming." Damien plunged a needle into Seth's bicep.

"Hey, heeeey," Seth said, his voice sounding far away.

"Look pig farmer don't make me strip you myself. You maybe my sister's type but you're not mine." Dr. Damien dropped the cordial act.

Seth pulled off his T-shirt. A little voice at the back of his brain told him to fight and keep his clothes on. *Where was his knife?* That voice faded to a pleasant drone telling him everything was perfect and of course he should take his overalls off.

Dr. Damien helped him take a tentative step into the water. Mud squelched up from between his toes and the pond was surprisingly warm, almost bath temperature.

"Is there a hot spring feeding this pond?" Seth heard his voice ask.

"Yay maybe. Who knows? Now get in. We swam in this pond as kids all the time. You're going to be just fine," Damien said.

Seth squinted and tried to think. *Swam as kids?*

"Get in!" Damien gave him a little push.

Seth slipped on the mud and landed in the pond with a thump. The buzz in his head increased. He sank into the warm water, leaving only his head unsubmerged.

"Did you actually think I was a doc? I should get an Oscar. I'm not sure what Dolores sees in you, but what she wants she gets." Damien walked back into the bush.

Dolores? His farm sitter and flirty neighbor? Seth looked up at the trees where the reddish ball of the sun was dropping behind the pine trees. He enjoyed the shifting pattern of light on the leaves. His eyes closed.

There was a light tickling on his arm, he squirmed, trying to stay asleep.

"Leave me alone, I don't want to get up yet."

The tickling persisted, but now he could feel it on his neck, and chest.

"Come on. Let me sleep."

He was so pleasantly warm, napping in this silky pond.

Wait.

Why was he sleeping in a pond? Braving the sunlight, Seth opened his eyes and he could see a dark spot on his cheek. A lump of mud. A twitching lump.

Adrenaline woke him fully and he jumped out of the water. He looked down at his arms, his mind not comprehending. The mud was lumpy, shiny and wiggling. He took one unnaturally thick hand, covered in the brown tubes and brushed at his opposing forearm. Globs fell; but not the ones directly against his skin.

It. Was. Not. Mud.

He was covered in leeches. Raising a black hand to his face, he could feel his cheeks, hilly and slimy. He tried to scream, but his tongue was too thick. Leeches clinging to his gums, his tongue, the sides of his cheek. A weak gargle and he swiped at his face desperately. He smashed his hands on his legs, searing pain when he managed to knock a few off.

Flinging himself onto the grass, he rolled and thrashed. His blood mixed with the torn leeches on the ground. Seth tried to draw air, straining to get his jaws open wide enough to breathe around the leeches in his mouth. He spit out bits of leech he'd gnashed with his teeth. *What a horrible metallic taste.* He stopped his desperate swiping and paused to get his strength back. There were still hundreds attached to his skin. Those that had survived his frantic tearing were visibly enlarging.

Two cool hands reached under armpits and helped him sit up.

"My handsome hunk, you'se best just relax now. This hard part be over soon." Dolores whispered in his ear.

Seth shoved her, but her long thin arms were strong and held him tight.

"Look, this is gonna make you better. No diabetes, no sicknesses, no more," she said.

"What have you done?" Seth mumbled around the leeches still on his tongue.

He could feel her hot breath on his infested neck. Her pink hair brushed his cheek.

"You are being overdosed with somethin called Hirudin. It's in leech saliva and it's gonna be making your blood super thin. And these ain't no normal leeches, they some special leeches. Give you super powers, like me and my bros."

"Special, how?" Seth asked.

My grandpa, who had a trailer on this here land used to talk about a secret nuclear test station, somethin must a leaked, I reckon, nuclear waste super juice." Dolores stroked his head, his thick hair pulling away in her fingers.

Nuclear leeches? He was too exhausted to react. The creatures fell off Seth's skin when full. Dolores reached into his mouth to pull them off his tongue; stroked his chest; and even reached into his underwear to gently remove the suckers attached there. She brought out a water bottle and he gulped gratefully. He felt a surge of strength and bliss as the liquid glopped down his throat. *It wasn't water. Was it wine? It was thick, tasted coppery...*

Seth spit out the liquid in his mouth. "What's in that bottle?"

"Why blood, hotty pants," Dolores said.

"What do you mean blood?"

Why did he feel so good? Strong, flexible, vital. Like he didn't need an ornate knife with lampreys carved in wood. He could fight with his bare hands.

He looked in wonder at his palms. An invisible slit opened and many little teeth glinted and gnashed from the center of each hand.

"Y'all like us now. A leech person. Damien, Dan and I swam in that there mudhole as kids, and we've been part leech ever since. I needed myself some non-related companionship."

Seth clenched his fists and the sucking mini mouths closed. Reaching up to his skull he pulled away big hunks of black hair.

"Ever see a leech with hair? Yup. You'll be bald. But strong, it's gonna be wonderful, I done wanted you for my man for ages."

Dolores smiled at him, super white teeth mocking him, the wrinkles around her lips stretched wide. Opening her thin arms, she walked towards him. "Come give me a hug you gorgeous sucker."

A wave of disgust, energy, and something else; something feral; raced through his body. Seth leapt up on strong sinewy legs and ran into the thick of the forest. Running like he hadn't since his high school days. No pain in his feet, no pain in his joints.

"Seth, waaaait!" Dolores called.

He didn't wait. He ran. He was hungry.

ABOUT THE AUTHOR

Angelique Fawns loves to spin dark tales and is incredibly nosy. She takes her natural inclination to ask far too many questions and interviews publishers, editors, and authors for horrortree.com and her own blog at www.fawns.ca/blog.

She has a day job as a television producer and lives on a farm north of Toronto with her husband, daughter, horses, cows, goats, chickens and a rescued Potcake dog.

When she can find the time, she sneaks away to her Golden Falcon trailer by the river to do some writing. You can find her work in *Ellery Queen Mystery Magazine*, *DreamForge Anvil*, and on her podcast *Read Me A Nightmare*.

facebook.com/amfawns

x.com/angeliquefawns

instagram.com/angeliqueiswriting

BUT WAIT! THERE'S MORE.

Enjoyed this book? Check out the others in the Horror Lite Series!

Cursed & Creepy

Peculiar Pets

Like to listen?

Read Me A Nightmare Podcast

Did you enjoy reading these dark quirky tales? Would you like to hear them performed on a podcast? Look for *Read Me A Nightmare* wherever you get your podcasts.

A writer yourself?

The Guide of All Guides

To learn more about selling your short stories and making money, I've created a guide to the best no-fee paying markets.

The Guide of All Guides is a comprehensive list of publishers and podcasters buying speculative fiction, complete with secrets and insights.

****Sign Up for my newsletter at www.fawns.ca*

If you enjoyed the foreword of this book, and "The Shadow Men", I highly recommend you check out Mark Leslie's series **Canadian Werewolf.**

https://books2read.com/b/bP56xJ

CAUGHT BETWEEN THE MOON AND NEW YORK CITY

Being a werewolf isn't all about howling at the moon.

Or running carelessly through boundless fields feeling the wind in your fur.

Not when you live in the most populous city in the US.

For Michael Andrews, a Canadian living in Manhattan and afflicted with lycanthropy, there are odd side effects to being a werewolf in the middle of a bustling metropolis.

Such as waking up naked in Battery Park with absolutely no memory of the night before as a wolf and trying to figure out why there is a bullet hole in his leg.

Just another day in the life of a man living with the odd side effect of his werewolf affliction.

9 781738 156610